In the Eastern Church, a Female Pope reigns but it is not Lady Challis. It is the one she knew as Cardinal Sophyra.

Pope Sophyra is a vampire, unlike like Lady Challis. Lady Challis, like a vampire from Hollywood, bites with fangs to inject the essential enzymes that allow her to feed, enslave, or kill. Cardinal Sophyra is a previously unknown species of vampire; she spits her enzymes or "venom."

When it lands on the victim, it seeps through the skin into the blood stream. Powerful, intelligent, and scheming, she and her kind not only drink the blood of humans, they harvest the bodies of their victims to feast on.

As Lady Challis and her daughter Elect-Si work to control Pope Sophyra, a third species of Vampire appears. Much closer to Pope Sophyra and the church's hierarchy, the agenda of this third species compromises the plans of Lady Challis and Elect-Si all at a time when the essential veil between the world of spirits, souls and our physical world is becoming thinner and thinner.

I0550066

## 1.	Moon Bathing

Elect-Si extended her right foot, pointing the toe of her knee-length black boot. Her stiletto heel seemed such a small surface to land on! All around her the moon caused the metal beams of the shattered roof to cast harsh angular shadows on the black dust that covered everything.

At the corner of her eye, something caught her attention.

A pigeon, frightened by her appearance, and maybe sensing her predatory being lurched suddenly into flight; it looked at her nervously as it dropped away from its perch and out in the direction of woods nearby. In the cold white light of the moon, she could see the loose black dust it had stirred up hanging in the air.

She licked her lips with the tip of her tongue; she would have to glide further into the building to avoid leaving a plume of dust in the air. She changed the angle of her wings and continued to glide. Slowing, she had a few treasured moments to look around for a good place to land, somewhere where she would be hidden when she touched down. As she scanned the remains of machinery on the floor, the decrepit state of the place became all too obvious.

Finally, she felt her heel touch down. Oh, so very soft she thought, flawless. As her second foot touched the concrete, she folded her wings away.

She squatted for a moment behind a large piece of machinery and looked around. The floor was broken at the eastern end; there must have been a large explosion on the ground floor that lifted and shattered the concrete. Reinforcing bars pointed upward like a grotesque, broken whicker basked.

She turned to the western end. A gaping hole was left where a large bank of extraction fans and glass panels had blown out. They had once sucked out the fumes from whatever they made inside and let in light for this upper-level machine shop. She looked back at the eastern end; the wall further along had a gap in it to the outside. She could fit through if her wings were in a tight, tucked position.

She liked multiple escape routes. A small breeze blew up at the western end. Her sharp vampire eyes spotted movement in the air. As she watched, the breeze ruffled a fine mesh of man-made fibre. It glittered in the harsh white moonlight. The web was incredibly fine but looked very strong; it was made to ensnare a vampire taking flight and cut their precious wings.

Standing, she shook her head and felt her long waist length black hair in its tight braid and carbon fibre hair clips slip back and forth across her back. Nothing out of place.

Another breeze, a different direction, it moved lazily along the outside of the building and in through a blown-out window. It was light and delicate in its strength, just like the one that had revealed the trap but this one brought a strong, pungent, gut clenching smell. She felt her stomach tighten, and she felt sick.

Human excrement, a lot of it, untreated, in the open. For a moment, she pinched her nose as she thought of the number of humans that could produce so much. Hundreds, perhaps thousands, but over time, not all at once. It had fermented to produce this stench. Then she detected the scent of decomposing human flesh. She moved to a shattered window, but stood back a little so that she could not be seen from the ground, and looked out. She had studied aerial imagery of the entire shabby complex and before landing she had circled several times, careful to hide herself in the dissipating fog and low cloud to confirm her studies. Nowhere had she seen any large-scale open cess pits or rotting human corpses.

She turned and bent down to pull up her knee boots and slipped her silenced machine pistol out of its holder and turned off the safety. On the left pocket of her jacket, she checked the status of the body cam. What happened here would be recorded. As she did, she became aware of small sounds. Hushed voices. Whispering. So, faint, so distant, she could not understand what was being said but there was a fierce sense of caution to the hushed whispers. A small voice. A child.

Elect-Si moved across the floor to the stairs.

The stairs were badly broken, in places only the metal rebar was left. The wall next to the stairs was pock marked by a huge number of bullet impacts. There must have been a stand of some sort by these stairs. Defenders on the upper floor trying to prevent attackers coming up. She stepped out and fluttered the tips of her wings, allowing her to glide through the still air to the floor below. Being a vampire does have its benefits, she thought. As she stepped on the floor, she moved quickly to one side and looked around to see if anyone saw her arrive. There was no one.

The hole in the upper floor was matched by a hole on this level. The explosion must have happened in the basement. She looked up to the roof; blast exits gaped to one side and a perfect round hole. The blast had blown off roof vents and large pieces of roofing. The round hole showed where a bomb passed through. It had penetrated this floor and the one above, where she had come and finally detonated in the basement.

She watched the moonlight playing across the ripped roofing material. No sign of a mesh there, another exit, perhaps a better one.

She looked around, Amunet was standing off to one side staring at her hands, the palms were covered with black dust, she must have touched something and was glaring at Elect-Si as she tried to rub it off. In return, Elect-Si shrugged and pointed to the gaping hole in the floor.

Amunet frowned but Elect-Si could feel a gentle breeze lift her and take her to the abyss. She pointed to the floor at one side of the bomb crater and held her machine pistol in front of her as Amunet took her down to land where it was safe.

The whispering was slightly louder now. The corridor to the right. The floor was covered in glass and smashed rubble. She started to walk very lightly and almost glide along so as not to tread on anything that might give her away.

She came to a pair of doors set back from the corridor wall. The recess must have saved them from being broken by the blast which had raged down the corridor. From between the gap in the doors, whispering beckoned, it was loud enough that words were almost decipherable.

Gently she pushed the door on the left; her machine pistol preceded her as she passed through.

The floor here seemed cleaner, swept, dull old-style incandescent lamps glowed from ceiling fixtures. Elect-Si took a couple of quick breaths; the wretched smell was overpowering here.

Words, she could understand words in the whispering now. A woman talking to a child that would not sleep. Another cautioning a son not to do what he planned. The child's voice is sullen in its hesitance at doing nothing.

Footsteps. A nun. The familiar black robes with red edging, she emerged from a door to Elect-Si's left but turning away from her, neither saw the other. The red edging denoted she was one of Sophyra's most obedient followers. A harvester of humans.

Elect-Si moved quickly to where the nun emerged and turned into it. The whispering was very loud now. More doors to the left, right, and straight ahead. She looked down at the floor to study the foot prints and pushed the door to her left cautiously. The smell of human blood and rotting flesh was immensely strong. She moved through the door and hid to one side.

For a moment, she closed her eyes, then opened them and looked around; no one had seen her. She made sure the safety catch on her machine pistol was off and stepped forward.

"Never again … close your eyes like that," whispered Amunet at her side.

Elect-Si felt the tackiness of the floor as she walked; it was bare concrete, but she knew why it was that way; it was all around them. Blood. Human blood. Row after row of humans, naked and dead, hung by their ankles their throats and wrists slashed, they had been left to bleed out into long urinal troughs. Each corpse is highlighted by its own personal incandescent bulb.

At the end of a row, the trough emptied into a plastic construction pipe. At a hole crudely hacked in the far wall, the pipes were joined to a larger one that disappeared out of sight.

As Elect-Si walked, her vampire senses told her the humans were grouped according to blood group. As they got further down the gruesome room, she realized the grouping was subdivided by race and age. Now the dead were children, no older than 10.

"So young…" whispered Amunet staring at the face of a girl.

"Puberty. This is where the special-order prepubescent blood is coming from." Murmured Elect-Si.

As she turned away from the last row, she saw the dissection tables. Extending to the far end of the floor, row after row of metal gurneys with wheels bolted to the floor littered with bodies.

"This is where they harvest the organs." She felt a breeze pass her and saw Amunet at the door to another room, beckoning Elect-Si.

"The vacuum packing line has broken down. Some of the bodies are rotting."

"That may be. But you are not a vampire. Organ meat is a bit like cheese; I don't like the smelly blue cheeses, but some people do; some people like their organ meat slightly decayed. But this has gone too far."

Amunet walked to some large packing crates filled with rows of sealed vacuum bags.

"I never thought of humans as cheese." She stooped to read the labels on the crates.

"This one is testacies, oh, and this one, ovaries." She straightened up, apparently surprised at the contents and then continued down the row of crates.

Elect-Si followed but more intent on the door at the far end. The sound of voices drew her like a magnet. As she passed

Amunet, she raised her machine pistol, which drew Amunet's attention away from the crates.

As she cautiously turned into the corridor, she saw stairs and moved up them quickly, and silently. Elect-Si came out on to a platform and moved back into the shadows.

Beneath her, row after row of metal cages containing partly clothed humans, 60 or 70 to a cage. The cages were all enclosing, sides and top, made of strong steel bars welded where bands crossed. The humans inside were grouped by age, gender, and race. Somehow it was as horrific as the room they had just left. At one end of each cage were bare metal toilets with no privacy screens, the sewage waste flushed out into open channels gouged into the floor with Jack hammers. From there it drained away through holes hacked into the walls. Cages containing women and children seemed less crowded. Males were packed tightly together and there was some pushing and shoving, as the stronger ones enforced more space for themselves at the expense of the weaker.

Somewhere underneath where Elect-Si was standing, a door banged open and she heard the clip of hard-souled shoes. Two nuns dressed in stylized black latex habits and head dresses appeared pushing gurneys with large, deep containers of steaming food. Behind, the nun Elect-Si had seen earlier stopped and surveyed the scene.

Several more nuns appeared. These had quite a different purpose Elect-Si surmised; they held restraints in their hands similar to the ones the cadavers were suspended from. These nuns would select humans to be taken into the next room, killed, and blood drained, then organs harvested.

At the men's cage, a nun had been taunting and encouraging a muscular young man to strip. Now naked, and pressed up against the bars, he had a very solid erection and she was enjoying making him publicly masturbate, as the other men in the cage looked on and yelled encouragement. The nun clapped and stepped back, pointing to the ground where she wanted the man to ejaculate.

Distracted for a moment Elect-Si did not see nuns with restraints opening the door of a cage with women and children. Somehow, they had failed to restrain a ten-year-old boy who was running desperately along a walkway between the cages. Elect-Si watched as the boy's mother was pushed to the ground, beaten, and electro shocked by two nuns.

The woman screamed as she was shocked. Her body lay across the cage opening, which caused other women and children to escape, all pressing forward and trying to get through the opening. Two more nuns rushed to the opening and used their shock rods to stun women and children and stop the escape.

The boy's frantic run changed everyone's focus to his escape. The nun who had been encouraging him whirled and squatted, pulling out an electroshock rod as she did. To Elect-Si, her face seemed to be bleached white, her lips very red and the makeup on her eyes a stylized Techno age very in vogue amongst nuns at the moment. The tip of her shock rod glowed red and she reached out for the boy as he ran past her but missed, which raised a loud cheer and banging on the bars of all the cages.

Elect-Si's attention immediately turned to the nun with the red-edged robe. She was moving to one side and from under her cloak she pulled out an automatic pistol. There was a brief moment of silence in the cages, only the boy's boots pounding on the floor could be heard, then the pistol muzzle erupted in a burst of fire.

The boy seemed to be carried forward in the air by the bullets ripping through his body. He made one grotesque attempt at another step but he was already dead; he crashed face first into the floor.

Silence for several moments, then the boy's mother screamed and struggled against the nuns to try and get to her son but several shocks to her legs robbed her of their use and she was thrown back into the cage and the door banged shut and locked.

Elect-Si spied a man, mostly hidden in the darkness of the doorway the boy had been running toward. He was raising an automatic weapon and emerging from behind the safety of the wall. No! Screamed Elect-Si's mind. No, you will die. As he brought the weapon up, she heard the automatic pistol bark its savage sound and bullets ripped into the wall next to the man and into his left arm and shoulder, spinning him around and bringing him fully out into the light. He fell to the floor on his back; he rolled over and fired his weapon but he had no control over it and bullets slammed into the nun by the men's cage.

The nun fell on the floor writhing and rolled around screaming. The young man she had been taunting suddenly ejaculated on her face.

The automatic pistol barked again, depriving the wounded man of several fingers of his right hand and blasting his weapon away from any possibility of his regaining control of it.

There was a blur of action as the nun's dispensing food ran to the side of their fallen sister. One had towels to stop the bleeding. The nuns who entered with restraints sprinted forward to the fallen gunman.

From out of the blackness, an angry burst of fire emerged from the weapon of a second man. The blaze of light from his weapon allowed Elect-Si to see the uniform of a local military policeman. Another burst of fire and two of the running nuns fell dead. The restraints she had been carrying skidded across the walkway in the direction of the fallen gunman, who was trying to crawl back towards the doorway, and his comrade, who came into the light to try and help him.

The nun with the automatic pistol stood unnervingly still and took careful aim.

The dying scream of the nun by the men's cage caught the others off guard and a burst of fire from the new gunman killed a third nun who slammed into the floor.
The black automatic pistol barked again. Its bullets hit the second gunman in the stomach and pushed him back a step. His back hit the corner of the door and he started to fall. A second burst of fire from the pistol ripped into his chest and neck. He slumped in a pile, dead, blocking the exit for the first gunmen staggering to his feet. Seeing the exit blocked, he slumped back on the floor resigned to his fate.

Silence. Then, the weeping sounds of the boy's mother broke the stillness. For a few moments, a stream of screaming and pounding on the bars of the cages erupted.

Half a dozen nuns appeared. They rushed to retrieve their fallen sisters and the dead by the men's cage.

More gurneys appeared and several nuns crowded around the fallen gunmen. Like the waters of the Nile parting before Moses, the nun who shot the men stepped forward and gave direction as she put away the pistol under her robes. Elect-Si listened carefully, cutting out the noise from all around her. The one still alive was to be taken away and they would try and save him, at least long enough for him to give up how he knew where to come and how he smuggled a message to the boy to try and escape.

As she turned to look at the men's cage, Elect-Si could clearly see a face, Dorion! Face pale, unnaturally so but young, the rumour was just 21, maybe even 20 but she wielded power cruelly and efficiently. Her eyes were blood red, lips slightly pouty and highlighted with black lip gloss. A red ruby glittered at the corner of each eye. Nails, blood red and very long, narrow, and pointed. The nail on the first finger of each hand was longer than the others and decorated with gem stones, which glittered like diamonds and rubies…

Now Elect-Si could see the robes clearly. The edging was intricate, beautiful lace dyed red and attached to the hem, cuffs and around the hood of her cape. The hood Dorion was now adjusting and was lined with red silk.

Dorion walked towards the naked young man held against the railing. He had been dragged out of the men's cage, put in restraints with his arms bent backward over his head.

Dorion moved close to the young man, who seemed frightened and terrified at one moment but willing to move toward her as much as the restraints allowed. Her cloak slipped back and Elect-Si could see Dorion's left hand had a firm grip of the young man's penis, which appeared to be stiffening. The pale hand with its long nails moved to his scrotum, massaging and tugging playfully at it. The long nails scratching and digging at it, stiffening the erection even further. His face contorted with sexual pleasure and a sense of unreality that his body was betraying his fear.

The young man suddenly froze, his body stiff and rigid, his knees weakened. He threw back his head and screamed that made the prisoners go silent. If they could watch from their cages, they saw the young man slumping, squirming, screaming over and over, feet thrashing on the floor in their hobbling restraints. Dorion turned and dropped something bloody on a gurney.

She turned and strode briskly to the exit. Elect-Si could see she had a black-bladed dagger in her other hand; blood dripped from it. Behind her, the nuns removed the restraints and beat the young man with their shock rods to make him walk, his legs glistening with blood spilling from his mutilation. Elect-Si's lips drew into a thin line as she realized what Dorion had dropped on the gurney was the man's testicles.

Elect-Si started to turn away from the scene but felt Amunet's hand on her arm.

"Not that way, turn right; there is a passage. It leads downstairs."

From the shadows, Elect-Si watched the nuns going about their business. Dorion directs everything in a brisk business, like emotionally detached manner with a small, soft, childlike voice.

The body of the dead military policeman and the boy were already hanging by their feet over troughs. Elect-Si watched dispassionately as a nun slit the throat of the child, then the man. Blood surged into the trough; for a moment, it made splashing sounds then it changed to a rapid dripping sound as the body drained and the plastic pipe emptied the trough efficiently.

Dorion turned her attention to the naked young man she had just castrated; he lay unconscious on a gurney, his legs dangling over the sides exposing the bloody hole in his body. Two nuns worked with surgical tools to seal it. When they were finished, they threw the instruments in an autoclave and slammed the door shut. As he was wheeled away, Dorion followed.

A nun entered pushing a gurney on which rested the still living military policeman; he groaned and held his broken and shredded hand in the air as blood dripped off his left hand on to the floor.

Elect-Si felt Amunet's breath as she whispered in her ear.

"I will go and play with the plastic curtains down the corridor."

Elect-Si brought her right hand around in front of her and nestled the pistol grip in her left as she raised it to eye level. As the plastic curtains began to rustle and shake, the nuns turned to look at the sound, allowing her to step out from the darkness.

The silenced machine pistol breathed sensually. The first three bullets ripped into the upper chest and throat of the nun who had just arrived. The force of the bullets tipped her over backward and her head hit the floor before the rest of her body. The second nun was still looking down the corridor as three rounds obliterated her neck and back of her skull; her body performed an elegant but odd pirouette, her robes swirling like a dancer around her before she smashed face first into the floor. The last nun opened her mouth to raise the alarm but a round hit her throat and two more into her face and she flipped over backward into the wall.

Elect-Si moved quickly to the gurney, looking up and down the corridor to make sure no other sisters would appear. As she looked down at the military policeman, he strained his head to one side to look at his colleague and the child. The blood was now drained from their bodies. Soon their corpses would be empty.

"Please number." He struggled with the words and the pools of blood on his body shimmered in the light.

Elect-Si nodded.

"Yes. I know." As she finished speaking, her fangs slipped out of their groves in the roof of her mouth and she leaned over and bit him on the neck. As the enzymes mingled in his body, the policeman shuddered several times, then went still.

As she straightened and stepped back, Amunet joined her and looked down at the dead nuns,

"I have their souls." A thin line crossed her lips.

"They have been harvesting humans here … like this, for over two years." She turned to look at the policeman, without a word and no apparent effort a column of air slid under him and lifted him from the metal gurney. Amunet gestured to the darkness where Elect-Si had hidden and together they moved into it and then out through an old side door.

2. Cabinet Sauvignon and Blood

Lady Challis gathered her robe around her and sipped at the intense mix of Cabinet Sauvignon and blood. The nail gloss on her toe nails was drying nicely. The red gloss was turning a deeper, darker, and very much richer colour.

Soon, it would be dry and the change in shade would reflect the richness and depth of colour from the blood she had mixed in her wine.

She dialled the lights in her room down so they barely registered at the edge of her balcony. Outside the waning moon cast its white light her flowers and plants in their planters and away in the distance, across the reflecting lake, the sounds of exotic night birds drifted in.

Lady Challis's eyes became fixed, fiercely intent on a scene she had seen many times, and held her breath. Her daughter, Elect-Si, was coming in to land. Her body upright, her legs moving as if she were walking in midair.

Finally, she extended her left foot, holding the right back and tucked underneath her. The rich cobalt blue wings glistened in the moon light. Lady Challis leaned forward in her chair. Elect-Si started to compress the air in front of her, slowing the glide and then, with several quick, powerful, braking pulses, stopped all forward motion, leaving her for a moment hanging in the air. Suddenly her outstretched foot touched the stone balcony railing of her suite. Her right leg came from under her, allowing her to elegantly step down, folding her wings as she did. A shower of petals from the plants at the edge of the railing cascaded slowly on to the balcony behind her.

Lady Challis exhaled, and reached for her wine glass and sipped.

"Did you watch the video?" asked Elect-Si as she swept into the breakfast room, a loose-fitting summer dress moving gently around her.

Lady Challis looked up and half turned to blow her daughter a kiss.

"Why do you insist on wearing stiletto heeled boots when you are flying? You maybe immortal but you can still break an ankle or a leg if that thin heel snaps when you land."

"I thought we settled this … that is what I am comfortable wearing." Elect-Si picked up a plate and stood next to her mother but looked at the scrambled eggs and bacon she was loading on to her plate along with other English breakfast delicacies. She picked up a strip of bacon from the silver serving platter and bit off a piece. As she did, she turned to her mother.

"So, did you watch the video or not?"

"I am your mother… I have a right to be concerned. I have a right to tell you things like that." Said Lady Challis, her voice firm and clear.

Elect-Si studied her mother's face and then leaned forward and kissed her on the cheek.

"I know and I appreciate it, I really do, and I understand what, and why you are saying what you do." She looked at her mother.

"You have bacon grease where I kissed you … sorry." She turned and moved to the breakfast table, one of the servants holding a chair out for her, while another filled a large ceramic mug with steaming black coffee.

Lady Challis allowed herself to be guided into her seat and picked up a napkin and wiped her daughter's kiss from her cheek.

"Yes, I watched the video. So that is one of Sophyra's processing factories?" Lady Challis picked up her knife and fork and studied her food.

"She always makes it sound so clean and sterile. The last time we met, she said the humans were already dead when they arrived. They were bodies diverted from funeral homes and morgues. Accident victims. She didn't say anything about what was in the video."

"Listen to the way she talks about them; they are like crops to her. The human race is like a field of wheat … fruit on a tree, or fish in the sea. She sends out Dorion to catch … herd … and then kill them. Bleed out the bodies, then cut them up for organs." Elect-Si looked at her mother's finger nails. The deep richness of colour betrayed her how it had been achieved.

"There was never enough blood to use for trivial things like enriching the colour of nail enamel." She gestured with her knife at her mother's hands.

"Now there is."

Lady Challis looked down at her fingers and the rich deep colour a few drops of blood had added to the enamel produced a rich sense of abundance. She wriggled her fingers; she was not sure whether she was looking at the attractive, mysterious colour or whether she was hoping it would somehow magically fall off, leaving her nails natural and clean. In silence, Lady Challis continued to eat.

"Who was the Military Policeman you bit?"

"He found out about the people caged there but did not know the purpose. The second policeman was to be a witness."

" … the child, who tried to escape?"

"I have no idea; he was not part of the plan."

"The mesh you detected over the obvious escape route, do you think they knew you were coming? You had an easy entrance but once inside the obvious escape paths were sealed in a way intended to stop someone who could fly?"

Elect-Si picked up two strips of bacon and folded a butter-laden piece of toast around them.

"I think it was intended for someone trying to enter the building rather than leaving it. Amunet told me she could have torn it down quite easily if I had asked." As she finished speaking, she bit down on the bacon sandwich.

Lady Challis sat quietly, her hands resting on the end of her chair arms, watching Elect-Si finish eating.
"I feel responsible." She paused and waved a servant to refill their coffee cups.

"I should have understood more about the desires of her genre of vampire and their tastes…. There were rumours, like swear words scrawled in a public toilet, but I did not pay enough attention." She fell silent.

"We have been over this before. Don't worry, Wellington has been going through all the records, and Burkhardt thinks he may have an analysis of their enzymes."

Lady Challis looked up at her daughter.

"… and?"

"Their species may be a lot younger than we believe. When Ferdinand and Isabella created the Tribunal of the Holy Office of the Inquisition in 1478, and let it loose on Spain and other Catholic countries, Expecting it to burn and torture heretics and other demoniac people, they may have come into existence then." Elect-Si picked up her coffee cup and sipped the steaming liquid.

"Parents would cut out or pull out their children's fangs to prevent them from being discovered as vampires."

"The enzyme a vampire creates has to go somewhere, so they started spitting them. Now they can spit more than twenty feet." Lady Challis slowly folded her napkin and put it beside her plate.

"I remember those times, terrible times. I went into the shadows where vampires were cowering and rescued as many as I could. I saw the fangless children; it seemed such a horrible mutilation. I took them away and healed their mouths and helped them grow up but never saw one of them spit. I never gave a thought about where the enzymes would go without fangs to deliver them." Lady Challis looked up and around the room, dwelling on the images shimmering in the reflecting lake.

"You did what was necessary for our kind, all, of our kind. According to Burkhardt, because there were no fangs to puncture the skin and inject enzymes into the blood, the enzymes became more concentrated and adapted to being absorbed through the skin."

"I guess, as those children became parents, they defanged their children, and so it perpetuated the cycle until there were children born without fangs."

"You did not create them Mother; it was their response to the Inquisition. Some of the strongest enzyme strains come from the other inquisition periods in France and Northern Italy. Those inquisitions were controlled by the papacy." Elect-Si drained her mug.

"I never saw any fangless children at those times either. But to be honest, I never looked for them."

"From what you tell me, in Spain, you saw the children when they were three or four years old. Maybe the mutilation was carried out on older children or even teenagers, as they would be better able to cover it up."
Lady Challis moved back from the table and stood up.

"Well, it is done now; we can't turn back history."

"Where are we going?" asked Elect-Si.

"We... we are going to the shooting range. You are going to make sure I can be as accurate as you with that machine pistol of yours." Said her mother briskly.

3.   Healing in the Reflecting Lake

Amunet breathed out ever so slightly and the mirror surface of the reflecting lake ripped, causing the water to drift higher on the steps. The water temperature and peace all around were so perfect for her. She reached back and pulled her long black hair over her shoulder and carefully squeezed out the water from her. In the warm breeze and sun, it would be dry quickly. She looked down at her arms and her belly. They were already dry.

A few feet from where she sat on the marble steps Elect-Si surfaced and held up a coin she had retrieved from the lake bottom. She studied it and then flipped it to Amunet. Then she turned around to pay attention to the man floating naked on the surface behind her.

His face changed swiftly between expressions of intense pain and peace. Elect-Si gently took hold of his arm; he moaned as if her touch caused him pain. Elect-Si guided him closer to Amunet. As she moved him, Elect-Si could see the same small fish that had nibbled at the dead skin in that deep valley high in Northern Mongolia.

Today the fish nibbled at the dried blood and dead skin of the wounds he had suffered. Part of his right hand was missing; most of the rest of it was covered in sutures and the remains of dried blood. The fish were having a feast.

"He is looking a lot better." Whispered Amunet.

Elect-Si held him close to the steps,

"Yes, the lake was a great idea."

"No, I reminded you what those little fish can do to help heal a body." She studied Elect-Si, who was iridescent in a peacock blue one-piece swim suit; rather odd she thought because everyone swam naked here.

"Did Challis say anything?"

"She said my enzymes must be exceptionally potent. His body is struggling with the pace they are driving it to heal."

The man moaned and rolled his head from side to side.

"Petr?"

The name was a whisper and called out at the same time. Then he became still, and his faced stopped switching back and forth between pain and peace. It seemed as if he were sleeping.

"My name. Petr is my name." He coughed violently and Elect-Si held him close to the steps so she could support him.

"My spine … it is on fire." He screamed so loudly Elect-Si was visibly shaken but she held on to him and pulled him partly out of the water.

"My Name…" He fell silent for several minutes. Elect-Si beckoned some servants waiting patiently by the steps to come and help take him from the water.
"Sit him on the wide step with his back against the wall. Get a wheelchair." She ordered.

He looked broken, achingly tired and only now coming to terms with what had happened and what the outcome had been. He cradled his right hand in his left like a delicate small baby. Slowly, his eyes opened and he squinted at the bright yellow marble and the sunlight. After a few moments, his eyes were fully open as they adjusted to the brightness.

"My name is Petr, so was the other policeman who died. He was my brother. We were twins. We never felt the togetherness many twins say they feel but when he died, I... I did. It was like, like a knife went down the centre of my body and cut away half of it."

Slowly, he tuned his hand over to fully take in the missing parts of his hand and the surgeon's work.

"Those little fish seem to have done a good job," he said slowly.

"The police were not my full-time job; I patrolled only part-time, always with my brother. I spent most of my time as a watchmaker. I will have to see how well I can carry on."

Elect-Si was about to say something when the servants arrived with a wheel chair and started to carry him to it.

She turned to face the reflecting lake and for a moment she closed her eyes. She felt the grass of the forest under her feet and the sunlight filtering through the trees. Against one of the trees, her guide stood nonchalantly and smiled when he saw her.

Elect-Si looked up at the tall trees; the sound of bird song had replaced the terrible shrieking and screams that had greeted when she first came to the forest.

"So different."

Her guide nodded.

"It is you who have changed, and in changing yourself, you have transformed this forest."

She looked at him quizzically.

"A riddle?"

"No." He stood up from the tree and walked through the lush grass to face her. He stopped in front of her and seemed to be studying her face.

"The screams and cries you heard when you first entered this realm, those were dark spirits trying to scare and persuade you to join them. They felt the darkness … the vampire, in you, they thought you would be the same as them. They did not expect you to use it against them. Now … they know they cannot scare or persuade you." He paused, tilting his head to one side as if listening.

"They know you walk without fear of them, and that you are not like them. They have felt your power against them. Your powers have grown exponentially, even if you have not been here, or used them … yet."

Elect-Si looked around at the lushness and beauty. She would love to open her wings and fly through the dappled light and race the birds that weaved through the forest.

"I came here to thank the lake spirits for helping heal that injured man… Petr … he is a vampire now."

"They know why you are here, and they are grateful for the thanks you offer them. So am I."

"You?"

"I was chosen to be your guide because I have guided many white shamans in their long and difficult journey. But I have never guided one, such as you. Vampires die, they can be killed," he gestured with his hands,

"But not you. You have an endless life." He paused as if sniffing the air.

"You are unpredictable; it is a very, very great power." He started to turn away.

"You didn't expect me to use my darkness against the evil spirits, did you?"

"I had faith in you, I believed you would," he looked over his shoulder at her for a long moment and then moved his head slightly as if listening again.

"The black spirits … they did not. But neither did the white spirits. They all stood back from you. They waited. They were uncertain. Now, they watch, and are surprised, again, and again."

He grinned.

"You did not have to bite Petr, some sprits, both black, and white, expected you to kill him to ease his pain. The black spirits wanted you to inflict more suffering and death. The white spirits expected you to be true to your darkness. Biting Petr changed him from a human, to a vampire, yes, but in so doing, you gave him existence. He can complete is life's purpose now. In the lake, you were helping to heal him. That too was … unforeseen." He turned and started to walk away.

"Wait, I have a question."

"Your bite." He looked up to the tree tops.

"Your bite is infinitely more potent than any vampire that has ever lived. It is much more powerful than your mother's. It is dominant and fierce in the death it carries, but … it can be transformative," he looked down at the ground and then continued to walk away.

"Wait, I have a question."

"Yes." He stopped and half looked over his shoulder in her direction. He seemed to know what would come next.

"How do you know what I want to ask?" asked Elect-Si.
"I am your guide. The answer is yes … to your question; the answer is yes."

A breeze blew across Elect-Si's face and she felt the soft deep rich richness of her robe she was now wearing. She found her hands in the midst of tying a simple knot in her belt.

She looked down at the whiteness of the fabric. Her skin and her hair were already dry but coolness clung to her face, hands, and calves. The sun was starting to set; rich red, orange, and yellow were streaked across the slowly darkening sky, but at this time of year, it brought coolness.

Her mind contemplated how long she had been standing by the lake but came to no conclusion. In front of her, Gwendoline was walking on the water, seemingly oblivious to Elect-Si until she slowly turned and met her gaze.

"Do you like?" Gwendoline took the sheer black voile covering to her full-length grey satin dress.

Gwendoline glided across the water towards Elect-Si and as she reached the marble edge, she held out her right hand. Her cane appeared from somewhere to Elect-Si's left and Gwendoline took hold of the glowing crystal handle. Slowly, she reached out with the cane and placed the gold tip on the marble and then stepped on to it. She stared into Elect-Si's eyes,

"You are an inspiration." Then she strode up the steps to the top and stopped, turning around to look down at Elect-Si,

"But I cannot wear white… in the way you do." Then she turned back to the palace and walked away.

4.   White Moon Diamond Pendant

Elect-Si studied her reflection in the mirror and smoothed the waist band of her pleated white leather skirt. She swished her hips to make the black panels on the inside of the pleats show. As she moved, she ran her fingers over the ridges of her muscular abdominals and watched her breasts jiggle only slightly; they were held in check by the strong pectoral muscles. She turned to the jewelry box to her left and took out the sparkling white moon diamond pendant with its blood-red ruby tear drop.

The pendant was a symbol of her Blood Rite. She had knelt in front of her mother reciting the ritual as her mother passed it over her head. The most powerful vampires in the world had come to witness her ritual, but more than that, they had come to see Lady Challis in person.

She adjusted it between her breasts and considered going shirtless to the meeting … just for a moment! Then she reached for her black leather shirt with its single diamond button just above her navel. She adjusted the waist band of her white leather skirt so the ruby at the front was exactly below her navel. It would show dramatically as she turned her shoulders. Almost ready, she thought. Now for the awkward part. She picked up a very small red ruby and carefully pressed it against the centre of her lower lip. Nailed it! She smiled. It shone seductively against her black lipstick.

She slipped on her stilettos and adjusted the diamond hair clip at the bottom of her waist length black hair.
As she turned to the door, she held out her hand for her cane to come to her from its place by her bed. The cane was a rod of pure bronze with fine gold strands spiralling around it. It was not a chick cane, perhaps the thickness of a human finger. It had been polished so brightly that it radiated a warm golden glow. It housed Emma the spirit she

met in the upper world and whose arm she healed. It also housed spirits her Banjhākri had gifted to her.

The Banjhakri had carved the handle to be an elegant version of her folded wings. It was made from the thigh bone of a Yeti and wrapped in gold wire. A rare red diamond was mounted at the front of the handle. The diamond had been found in a stream by another Banjhakri who had donated to the cane.

Oops, one last touch. A vampire must never be without her dagger! She clipped its sheath into the links hanging from the waist band of her skirt.

5.   A Blood Rite

At the palace's ballroom door, she waited, slightly back from the entrance, looking at Burkhardt. When her mother gave him the signal, he would announce her and she would enter.

"So, are you coming to my room tonight?" she murmured.

"Of course," replied Burkhardt quietly. He turned his head to look appreciatively at her,

" … it has been too long since we fucked our brains out. I am looking forward to it."

As he spoke, he passed the mallet he would strike the large copper going with, from his left hand to his right, and straighten the wing collar of his shirt. He swung his right hand, unleashing it on a large copper gong. The sound made her jump; she had not expected Burkhardt to hit it with such force.

The murmur of conversation from inside the room abruptly stopped. Silence poured from the ceiling. Not a sound could be heard. Burkhardt took one pace to his right and one forward as he prepared to raise his voice and announce her; he held out his left arm as if he were directing traffic.

"Lady Challis, and all who have assembled here today." He looked at Elect-Si, the signal for her to step into the room.

"She, who is venerated in the Holiest of Holies. She who is blessed in The Most Ancient Blood Right. Daughter of Lady Challis. Vicereine Elect-Si," he paused, then added, "White Shaman." As he finished, he turned to look at Elect-Si, who had started to enter the room. He turned back to the room and opened his mouth and issued the command.

"All kneel."

Elect-Si moved a few feet further into the room and stopped. The room was bright and contained two hundred or more people; women dressed somewhat casually like herself and others had chosen to wear full-length ball gowns. The men, some in-military uniforms, some in high fashion suits. Others in a bow tie and tails, similar to Burkhardt.

Two servants offered her crystal glasses from silver platters. Behind her, the doors closed. Elect-Si took a glass and held it high in the air. She cast her gaze around the room, meeting the intense stares of everyone in the room.

Men and women sank to one knee and bowed their heads. Several remained standing, looking alternately at her, their glasses, and the vast majority of vampires now kneeling. She waited, one by one, they knelt if reluctantly in deference to her.

"I greet you. I toast you. I toast our kind and our purpose here tonight." Slowly she brought her glass down to her lips and sipped at the water. Then she raised it in a toast and started walking down the length of the hall to attend her mother standing on a raised dais.

She moved slowly, and deliberately alow9jg everyone to take in the moment, the occasion. From her left, a crystal glass arced through the air, landing a few feet in front of her and smashing into the Indian marble mosaic floor. The smashing of the glass broke the electric silence in the room, and splashed blood across several large tiles. To her left, another glass smashed on the floor, spilling its contents. It was followed by several closer to her mother. Elect-Si did not pause in her stride, but from the corner of her eye she could see the thrower of the first glass getting to his feet. Those who threw the other glasses were also starting to stand.

They were not honouring her. They would not survive the night.

As Elect-Si got closer to her mother, she could see a group of taller, stronger, more heavily set men. All dressed in black, they knelt in her honour but did not have glasses to toast with. In amongst them, like a strange red flower, Dorion!

Dressed in a red habit, she knelt as if in church, her hands together in front of her, the fingers with their pointed and painted nails wrapped around a fine crystal goblet of blood. The habit was slashed from hem almost to crotch at the front of each leg, revealing black stockings held up by a garter belt. The garter clasps in the form of a crucifix and studded with diamonds. Around her neck on a heavy gold chain, a gold crucifix. In the middle of the crucifix, a crystal containing blood from the first human she had killed.

Her shoulders were bare, revealing their alabaster whiteness. Set against the paleness a tattoo of a gothic crucifix with a bloody centre on each slender bicep. A sheer red veil was attached to her black coif.

As Elect-Si came close, Dorion looked up. The incredible white alabaster skin was starkly contrasted by red lips and the unnaturally bright red eyes. As their eyes met, Doiron's lips parted, her tongue appeared and seemed to hover in the opening, as if, like a snake, it was smelling the air. The tongue then took a slow, sensuous journey around her lips before disappearing back inside and her lips closed.

Elect-Si arrived at the step below where her mother stood and held her glass of water high up so that all could see it.

She brought it down to sip from before placing it on a servant's silver serving tray. Along the length of the hall, guests were standing and receiving new drinks from the many servants.

Dorion moved out from amongst her retinue and faced the hall holding her glass high.

"In the name of her Holiness Pope Sophyra, I honour Vicereine Elect-Si." She waited for those in the hall to sip their glasses and then turned to Elect-Si with her glass still held high.

Their eyes met; again, the lips parted slightly, allowing Elect-Si to see Dorion's tongue appear and abruptly disappear. As her lips closed, Dorion knelt again. The slits in her habit exposing her pale white thighs above her black stockings.

Elect-Si nibbled on the inside of her bottom lip as she fixated on those white thighs.

No! Screamed her soul!

As Dorion bowed her head, a new lustful thought entered Elect-Si's mind … if she only had her machine pistol, three rounds in the back of Dorion's head would be much more satisfying. Perhaps a round emerging on to the floor from each eye, and one through that pouty little mouth. Yes, thought Elect-Si—love the idea.

Dorion slowly stood up and sipped at her glass, her eyes locked on to Elect-Si.

"You visited one of my harvesting plants…" she paused but got no reaction.

"You killed three of my nuns." Still no reaction to her words.

"You stole a human we were about to process." Still no reaction. She sipped from her glass again and slowly turned away to be with her retinue.

Elect-Si sat back and studied her toe nails. Cleaning and repainting them with a different colour was almost finished; she was happy with the result. Opposite her, Miray sat on the floor of the balcony, her back against the marble balustrade, legs stretched out in front of her. She was unpicking the knot in her bandana and balancing her assault rifle on her thighs.

"It's important that those who disrespected you pay for doing so." Miray finally undid the knot and looked up as the material came loose. Their eyes met.

"It was your mother's wish that they be killed." Miray's stare held Elect-Si's eyes.

"How many did Dorion want dead as well?"

Miray looked down at the bandana she was refolding.

"I believe most of them. We turned eight into spies for us." She wrapped the material around her head and knotted it again.

"Good?"

"I don't think Dorion was using us to cull her followers. We interrogated them before we executed them. They hoped to ingratiate themselves with Dorion; they believed it was what she wanted. A few of their family members, who were not present cursed you and the ceremony when we visited them. They are dead also. The effect on Dorion's retinue is noticeable when she is in public." Miray looked up.

"There are more priests around her. They are all young, energetic, and rush to do her bidding."

"Energetic!" Elect-Si put the top on her nail varnish.

"Is she fucking them?"

"Yes. The word is they have all been castrated; she has their balls prepared by her chef and eats them in front of them."

Elect-Si grinned; perhaps that was the fate of the young man she had seen Dorion castrate. But her mind ran past the images of that night; it disappeared down a long dark tunnel into history. It arrived in a large open-air space lined with huge book shelves. Like a person frantically searching for an answer to a mystery, her mind pulled out books and threw them on a large table. Flipping them open as they landed, she scanned the pages for what she was looking for.

"She is forming a cadre of priests to administer the bureaucracy she requires for harvesting humans. She is replacing the old way of doing it." Elect-Si leaned forward and admired her toe nails. Her mind continued to scan the pages laid out in front of her mind.

"Make a connection with that group; we must start to exploit them. I want control of at least two, maybe three."

"Castration figured in a number of religious cults," said Miray.

"Should we start one amongst that group?"

Elect-Si stood up and ran her fingers through her hair.

"Make sure control of harvesting humans is given to one of the priests we have by the throat? But … we must not be connected with any of this."

Miray stood up and slung her assault rifle over her shoulder.

"I will make it happen… Good night."

6.   Gwendoline

Lady Challis pushed her tablet away and leaned back in her chair and looked up at the ceiling. After a moment, she closed her eyes and rubbed them, yawning as she did so.

"Tired, Sister? Or, should I ask, are you tired of what you are reading?" Murmured Gwendoline as she stared at the woman opposite her.

"I am tired of what I am reading," Lady Challis paused and straightened to look at Gwendoline.

"Humans have a saying about their eyes not being able to unsee things they find disgusting…" She pointed at the tablet screen.

"More videos at Dorion's harvesting centres. This time the Middle East. Do you want to look at them?"

"No." Gwendoline said curtly. She looked at her sister. In the eye.

"We went through the Inquisition, all of them. Enough!" she declared.

"Enough! And you were with the Mongol armies for many, many years. They were renowned for death and destruction." She looked down at the tablet,

"Is it any worse?"

"No, the same.' Lady Challis paused…
"Yes! Yes, it is much worse. The army killed but they never dissected the corpses and ate them. Neither did the Catholic priests of the Inquisition. I find it hard to understand the volume of organs and body parts processed." Lady Challis's head dropped slowly back to look at the tablet.

"Miray obtained a worksheet of sales and revenues...." Said Lady Challis yawning again as she passed the spread sheet across the table.

Gwendoline sipped at a glass of champagne with fruit floating in it. A smile passed over her lips as she scanned the printout.

"The zealots are using emasculators designed for horses and bulls on themselves," she said giggling. Then she looked at Lady Challis.

"They have a ceremony, ritual and a cult. Dorion will have a formidable group soon. Castrates tend to follow more obediently those who altered them." Mused Gwendoline looking out the window.

"Seventy. There are seventy in the cult." Gwendoline put the paper on the table and stood up, picking up her champagne glass she held it out for a servant to refill.

"What? Why that face? You can't call them the enemy. The church leaders around Sophyra are all her genres of vampire. This thing with Dorion makes money and lets them satiate their desires within the agreement we have with them."
"I didn't say call them enemies. They are equal and different. Sometime in the future, we may need their support and their numbers." Gwendoline flowered at Lady Challis.

"If someone opened your mouth and looked inside, they would see your fangs. Their mouth would look human, which is what we are trying to be all along but needed to keep our mothers shut at the same time," Gwendoline held up her glass for Lady Challis to toast with.

For a long moment, Lady Challis looked down at Gwendoline. Inside her mouth, her tongue flicked over her fangs and the channels they folded into. Slowly she moved her glass forward to chink against Gwendoline again.

"Yes, Sister, we are." Slowly she walked towards the day bed.

"Another thing to sleep on Challis. Loose the chip on your shoulder about them achieving twin papacies, in the East and the West. We have struggled with just one Pope for centuries. All out planning and scheming brought us here, now. Enjoy it." Gwendoline paused.

"They could not have achieved what they have without you, your plans and your vision across the centuries. Your scheming, the manipulation, and the murders. Be nice to yourself about those things." Gwendoline listened; the sound of Lady Challis's breathing betrayed her relaxed appearance.

7.   Phaedra

Phaedra leaned back in the chair so the priest standing behind could feel her breast and its hardening nipple. As she changed her position, she reached up and adjusted the heavy gold cross attached to her collar. On her knees a tablet showing a copy of the Religious Observance for Nuns.

Eyes blackened by glowing, luminescent makeup appeared to shimmer and mock painted tears dripped like stars from the corners of her eyes. She moved the slits in her habit so he could see more of her thighs.

"If it pleases your father, I learned three things." She said looking down and staring at her reflection.

"Go on Phaedra, tell me."

"The reflection I see of myself in the good book, what I am now and what I have become. What was in me before is gone, never to return." Phaedra waited.

"Go on."

Phaedra looked down at the digital book and turned several pages.

"I am not to show compassion or mercy to our enemies." She waited nervously; the needing motion was harder and deeper now. Her nipple stiffened.

"Good. Go on."
She took a deep breath.

"Everyone wants to be a wolf, a powerful predator, but not me. I do not want. Because I am the wolf. I do things a Wolf does, and I do them without mercy."

"Very good. That is all correct. Now. Are you ready?"

"Yes, Father, I am ready."

"Good."

She looked around the Audience room of the seminary. Most of the lights have been turned off or dimmed, except those shinning down on the floor between two rows of high-backed chairs. The chairs waited patiently for those who were to attend the ceremony. At the head of the room, on a dais two steps higher than the stone floor, a Cardinals chair from which was handed down decisions for all who came to be judged.

At the far end, tall wooden doors opened slowly on creaking hinges. One-by-one, priests entered and took up seats their opposite. None of them looked at her, or her beloved.

Several minutes passed, then, one by one, two lines of naked young men entered, walking barefoot on the cold stone, they were proud, and walked with shoulders back and chests out. Shaved heads were muscular and fit; They looked forward with unflinching gaze. Staring straight ahead, they walked with purpose, determination, and a mission. Phaedra bit her bottom lip; the men had all been castrated.

Between the two lines, one walked who was intact, as they say in animal husbandry. She recognized his face; this was the one she had selected from those exercising in the seminary courtyard. His face was blank, expressionless. But his eyes moved rapidly from side to side. His nostrils flared, giving away his heavy breathing.

Behind him walked more castrated young men but one who held in his hands, something she recognized. An emasculator. She had helped her father castrate several horses and bulls on their farm. She was familiar with the tool.

With no sons, she and her sisters had to help with all manner of tasks connected with the farm, deciding which stallion or bull to keep intact for breeding, and which to be castrated was a skill he taught her and she had used it this morning.

The group stopped short of the steps to the Cardinal's chair. The door closed with what seemed careless bumping and banging. Then, silence; the lighting brightened over the centre of the floor. From high above, a spot light of bright, cold white light scorched down illuminating the intact young man.

It seemed like an hour passed before one of the priests stepped down and walked over to him. It seemed to take an eternity; the priest was blessing the young man and spent several minutes speaking to him quietly. Then the priest suddenly reached up and took him heavily by the back of the neck and pulled his head down in one powerful motion. As he did so, he took a small squeeze bottle from his vestments and pushed a mask over the man's nose and squeezed. The young man let out a yell and struggled momentarily at the violent act and what had been squirted into his nose. Seconds passed, he maintained his standing composure, then his head rolled side to side and he stared up at the bight beam of light. Caught like a moth in the light, he wavered, his arms starting to move upward to the light as if receiving a blessing. Then he fell to his knees and then forward on to his hands.

Phaedra rose quickly and stepped down on to the floor, her stilettos making distinctive clicking sound on the stone. Her legs swishing out throw the slits in her habit. Just like the legs of a wolf on its hunt.

She stood next to the hips of the young man and looked at his cock and balls. As she stood there, a hand appeared and grasped the testicles, pulling them back and up. The motion and power almost lifted the young man off his knees. He grunted heavily and his arms struggled to hold him on all fours for a moment. Phaedra bit her bottom lip, just like a calf she had helped castrate before leaving to become a nun.

The emasculator appeared in her vision. She waited for a hand to place the testicles in the device and offer the handles to her. In her mind, the image of that calf's back, just like that of the young man, merged and she closed the handles abruptly.

The young man's head jerked up violently; he opened his mouth to scream but no sound came out. His hands started to slide on the floor and he fell forward, his forehead making a cracking sound as it hit the floor and he passed out. The rest of the body followed his face. As Phaedra waited for the emasculator to be taken from her, she watched the testicles disappear out of the corner of her eye. The four men closest to the sprawled body casually flipped him on his back and took hold of a wrist or ankle and carried him back to the doors which were opening slowly. A gaping wound between his legs bleeding thick drops of blood on to the floor.

Around the room, the priests stood, smiling, and applauded. One by one they stepped down and walked over to her. One turned and looked up at her beloved.

"Cassius, Phaedra is a wonder. So quick, and without hesitation. You are a very lucky man." One said.

Phaedra basked in the glow of their congratulations and thanked her father for the skill he had taught her.

Cassius locked the door and pushed Phaedra further into their love nest. She waited obediently for him to unzip her habit and push it off her shoulders. It fell to the floor, leaving her naked except for her crucifix, stockings, and stilettos.

He came from behind her, his arms wrapping around her, a hand taking hold of each breast.

"You have a new role in the seminary. They liked the way you selected that boy and cut off his balls." He paused and nibbled at her ear and then sucked on her neck.

Phaedra pushed back against him, rubbing her ass on his crotch. He needed her breasts as if they were dough and it was getting tiresome; today it hurt. She would rather he use his cock, and put it in her right away.

"They were watching me select him?"

"Yes." His hands dropped to her stomach just below her navel.

"It is time for you to be bred."

"Bred? You mean have your baby?"

"Mine, or Alessandro's. He has a desire to impregnate you."

"Alessandro is so … old. I would rather have yours," she murmured quietly and seductively. The idea of having Alessandro's old cock in her started to make her feel ill. "What you have been doing to stop having a baby has to end. If you don't get pregnant by the end of the summer, you will go to Alessandro. He is something of a stallion; he will surely breed with you."

Phaedra closed her eyes. The idea of her being something to be impregnated like a cow on the farm without any care or thought … disgusted her.

"What is my new role in the seminary?" The question distracted her away from the thought of babies.

"You will do all the emasculations." Cassius spun her around to look at her directly.

"That means you will start meeting Dorion on a regular basis to plan and strategize how the young studs brought here are managed. She is only just becoming aware of this rather unique group of young men and their potential."

"Is she aware you are the organizer?"

"She may, but I have never met her. I have never heard from her or thought that she knows of me. But I hope she does. You will have to make her aware of my leadership, what I have created and what I am offering her." He paused.

"Increase the number of emasculations." He looked over her head at the bed and its freshly made sheets.

"Five every day for the next two months…" His voice trailed off.
"I need what the old Romans called a century, one hundred. I want to present a century to her. I hear she likes tradition and history."

"What then?"

"Another century … perhaps"

"What are you going to do with them?" As she looked up at him, she worked quickly to undo his pants and push them down to the floor, where he stepped out of them. She gripped his stiff cock and massaged the testicles she would soon be removing from so many young men.

Cassius's eyes rolled in their sockets as he broke eye contact and inhaled sharply and deeply at his lust for her.

"Pope Sophyra needs to harvest more humans." He stopped and inhaled in halting deep breaths.

"The demands of her kind for blood and organs cannot be satisfied with the process Dorion has in place." Cassius looked down at his baby and nudged her chin playfully.

"Sophyra will start a small war using papal proxies. It will be contained and very limited, but the killing will meet demand. The young men we turn out here will be used to escalate the war, retrieve human body parts, and take prisoners that won't be missed in a war zone." He met her eyes, so enchanting he thought.

"Get on the bed, I need to fuck your brains out and cover your insides with my cum!" He kissed her.
"None of it in your mouth or ass from now on."

Phaedra watched Cassius's back disappear through the door and heard it lock. For a long while, she lay on the violently messed up bed until finally she heard a small pebble hit the wall close to her window. She frowned at the inaccuracy but smiled.

She rolled out of bed and opened the window, the sign to the person down in the garden that she had heard and would be coming down. No time to shower or properly clean herself. She slipped on a robe and walked to the door. For a moment, she stopped and listened. Carefully she slipped a brass key out of her pocket and opened the locked door. A quick look up and down the corridor to make sure all was clear and then she was outside the door and locking it. Barefoot, she was heading down into the garden.

Slowly she emerged into the garden and moved towards some thick, tall bushes but a small pebble landed at her feet from another direction. She turned and looked. An old barrel-chested man with a thick walking stick stood mostly hidden in another thicket. Moving along the wall, she quickly made it to the new hiding place.

She stood close to the old man, smelling the mixture of sweat and soil from the garden. She slipped the knot on her robe and let it fall open. For a long moment, there was no movement. Then the old man extended the handle of his walking stick to push the robe further aside, exposing her completely. His eyes glittered…

"He has been riding you like a mare…" their eyes met as he looked at her.
"I would rather it was you…" Phaedra murmured.

"I would rather it was me as well. But there will be time for that when things are the way we want them." He paused,

"Is it done?"

She stepped forward and pressed her body up against his sweat-stained shirt. She felt the stiffness of his cock in his pants. She kissed him hungrily for what seemed to be ages and then broke the embrace and stepped back, doing up the knot on her robe.

"Yes, it is done."

"Are you sure? You must be sure Phaedra. No doubts, no questions, no maybe. Certainty. You must be certain." His old voice was scratchy, but clear.

Phaedra held up her hands and extended her fingers as if she were admiring them. Slowly in the moonlight passing through the ticket, a colourless liquid formed at the edge of her nails and dripped into the soil.

"I am as sure as that."

The old man pursed his lips.

"You must break the skin, there must be a mingling of that liquid and his blood."

"Yes, I know. I am certain."

He nodded.

"I have news!" Smiled Phaedra,

"I am to do all the emasculations in the seminary; he wants five a day, every day for the next two months. Then he wants another one hundred … maybe. He says Sophyra will be starting a small war using papal proxies. Dorion will be able to harvest more humans under the cover of war. The castrated will be used for harvesting and to keep the war going." She stopped talking. A rustling in the thicket. Was it the wind, an animal or someone listening? The sound stopped and then the sounds of a small animal disappearing on the driveway.

"I will be meeting Dorion very soon. He wants me to make sure she knows him and what he has created. And what he plans."

The old man shifted his weight and snorted.

"Do what he asks." He shifted a small stone on the ground with his walking stick, "five men a day for the next two months, that is much more than a century. You must discover the true numbers, and especially how they will be used." He looked up at Phaedra's innocent upturned face.

"Find out. Make Dorion your friend, not his. She is a direct path to Sophyra."

"I must go back…"

The old man nodded and took a small packet from his worn gardeners' jacket.

"You will need this."

She looked at the packet, knowing its contents, the magic potion that stopped her from having babies. She reached out quickly and slipped it into her robe.

"If I do not get pregnant by the end of a summer, I have to go to a different priest." She looked up and met the old man's eyes.

"Alessandro, probably."

"Well, he is not as old as I am." A smile crossed his lips. He gestured at the swelling in his old pants,

"Get rid of this before you leave. Suck me!"

As Phaedra stood up, she wiped the corners of her mouth and pulled up the zipper on his pants. She smiled, their eyes met, but he gestured for her to leave.

She checked her robe and made sure it was closed and the knot was good. She turned away from him but did not take a step.

"If I don't have a baby with Cassius, and I am given to Alessandro, maybe we can work it that you give me a baby. We could let Alessandro think it is his." She half looked over her shoulder, waiting for his reply.

"That would be nice; we must plan it, though, as we plan everything."

There was silence for a moment…

"Phaedra, you are a good daughter, your father loves you."

"Thank you, Papa. I love you too." Slowly and cautiously, she parted the thicket leaves and walked away.

Phaedra sat with her hands clasped together in her lap. The slits in her habit showed her red stockings with their white lace tops and jewelled garter belt clasps. Between the noticeable shape of her breasts, the large gold crucifix reflected lights from large, open, seminary windows. On her head, she now wore the red koukoulion of Dorion's order. She met Dorion's gaze without flinching.

Dorion was laughing loudly, and had been for almost a minute. Her eyes switched from her tablet to Phaedra and back. She had been replaying the emasculation ceremonies of the previous day. The second to last had fixed her attention and she had replied to it over and over. A twinge of sympathy for the young man in the video passed Phaedra's lips but disappeared as quickly as it had appeared.

Dorion finally turned the tablet off and concentrated on Phaedra.

"So funny! Hilarious. I like what you have done, adding formality and titles to things that make it something other than it is." She turned to look out the window at the blue sky with just a few clouds in it.

"Ceremony, Honor Guard, and Treatment … very good."

She continued to look out the window for several minutes. Abruptly she turned back to Phaedra.

"Cassius. Is he trying to breed you?"

"Yes."
"You are not to breed with him. Do you understand?"

"Yes … but he says if I do not, I will be passed to another priest who will succeed."

"Hmmm… I hear Alessandro is considered to be quite a bull here; he is a dozen offspring already. Make sure he is next to receive treatment…" Dorion looked at her watch.

"I was not aware treatments could extend to priests; Alessandro was a senior in the Seminary." Said Phaedra.

"You are in my order now, nuns in my order are not for priests to use as they see fi, or to be bred by them. You can pass that message on to Cassius." She paused as if deliberating how to express her thoughts.

"Where did Cassius get the idea of creating such a force and gifting it to me?"

"I do not know. We were lying in bed a few months ago. He suddenly said he had a new role for me, then he explained it."

"And the treatments, you are perfuming them seven days a week, five a day?"

"Yes. For two months and then I am to repeat for another two." Phaedra sensed danger but decided the next words should be said; this was her opportunity to gain favour with Dorion.

"Cassius said he would present a century of men to you … but the numbers do not add up. If I keep to the plan, he told me, I would be performing more treatments than required."

Dorion looked down briefly and then back up at Phaedra.

"Has he said what he will be doing with the extra men?"

"No."

"Find out. Report to me! We must stay in regular contact, at least twice a week or more. A small number have been committed to the war; they are excellent fighters and ferociously devoted to the Pope." Dorion's voice trailed off.

"I dine with Pope Sophyra several times during the week; we exchange a lot of information. I will honour you by bringing your name to her attention." Dorion made the sign of the crucifix with her hand.

"The information you give me will be part of our conversation. Make sure it is clear and accurate. Everything that goes on here, with the ceremonies and the priests, I must know everything." As she walked past Phaedra's chair, she took a black leather box from her pocket and set it on the table in front of Phaedra.

Phaedra slowly opened it. Inside a gold crucifix glittered with rubies.

"Only those close to me have the right to wear a blood crucifix. That big gold thing you are wearing is so crude. I don't want to see it again."

Dorion stopped a few feet away.

"How we contact each other, how often … what we talk about… Cassius does not need to know. Understand?"

Phaedra looked up from the blood crucifix to Dorion, and nodded.

Dorion let herself out.

Elect-Si looked carefully at the back of the guard's head; a fresh haircut! The neatly trimmed hair line showing from just under the protective combat helmet. She aimed the tip of the silencer upward so as to have the bullet penetrate the brain and kill quickly. She pulled the trigger, flame erupted from the end of the silencer and a single round ripped into the back of the skull and simultaneously a volcano erupted on the top of the helmet. Fragments of Kevlar and lining shot into the air followed by a gush of blood and brain matter that seemed to hang in the cold harsh light of the surveillance lights for hours.

Before the body dropped to the ground, Elect-Si had a powerful grip on the straps of the bullet-proof jacket. She ripped the name tag from the guard's neck and dragged the corpse into the shadows. She took out her combat knife and slashed open the front of the soldier's pants to look inside.

Time was pressing. They were on a very tight schedule; she could not dawdle. She moved quickly and silently up the steps to the metal door and turned the handle. It was open. She slipped inside, followed by Petr and several of Miray's soldiers.

The temperature in the building was brutally cold. Perfect for storing vegetables, meat, and human corpses. She sniffed the air; she could smell them, a strong, sharp, odour. She slipped the selector of her machine pistol from single shot to burst mode.

She moved forward, but became aware after a few steps that Peter was not moving. She looked over her shoulder at him. He was transfixed, his nostrils flaring and compressing as he breathed deeply through his nose. She realized with surprise that she had not considered how smelling dead humans would affect him now that he was a vampire.

A burst of flame from silenced automatic fire erupted from Elect-Si's right. Her head jerked round to look in the direction of the tracer rounds. Two armed men had emerged from between tall warehousing shelves loaded heavily with pallets of vegetables. A burst of silenced gunfire from her team and the men fell in mid stride, mouths open but silent. But the loud gunfire meant the damage was done. One of Elect-Si's team moved to them with a knife to slit their throats and make sure they were dead. Then, oddly, it seemed to Elect-Si, pull down their pants to inspect the genitals.

The soldier looked in her direction and made a chopping sign with his hand before ripping the dog tags from the bodies.

Elect-Si moved over to Petr and punched him hard in the arm. He inhaled sharply at the pain as her knuckles compressed tissue all the way down to the bone. But he said nothing; he simply turned his head to follow her pointing fingers.

Petr squatted behind a heavy industrial weigh scale and waited at the door to the back of the freezer container to swing open. He shuddered at the sight. Stacked two pallets high, naked frozen human corpses, some with brutal damage to their limbs, and torso from gunfire or explosives.

Some corpses were all headless, but stashed against the side of the freezer container and a pallet was a large plastic bag of heads with grotesque faces pushed up against the clear plastic. At the bottom of the bag, a large pool of blood and clear cranial fluid frozen solid.

Another burst of gunfire, and two more guards fell dead. Elect-Si hissed at one of Miray's guards, who started to move forward to inspect the bodies, and slit their throats.

The soldiers stopped as Elect-Si took careful aim and sent three rounds into each body to make sure they were dead.

She turned to Petr and roughly took hold of his weapon vest and pulled him upright and turned him away from looking at the freezer container.

"Get the name tags."

The doors to the container were silently closed; as they closed, the container truck moved forward, breaking the seal with the cold storage facility. The movement left enough space for them to jump down and make their escape.

8.   Assessment

Miray sat behind a beautifully carved table from the Ming period. Laid out on top were parts and clips of bullets from her side arm. She studied each intently on the mirror-like wood finish.

"It happened. Will it happen again?"

All eyes turned to Petr, who sat scowling in a sleeveless T-shirt. A large black and purple bruise on his arm where Elect-Si had punched him.

"It was the first time I had smelled dead humans since changing. Now I know what they smell like; it won't happen again." He lifted a glass of scotch to his lips and sipped at it.

Elect-Si stood with her back to the meeting a glass of brandy in her hand, her cane standing close to her right leg. The tip is hovering a couple of inches above the floor. Lady Challis sat at a card table a few feet away, idly it seemed, turning over cards and occasionally looking up at the group to study the interaction between them.

From behind her, the sound of fine silk swishing on marble tiles and the soft padding of bare feet. Gwendoline moved to sit in a free chair and arrange her sari of gold and black with her familiar black lace. Her long white hair platted and hanging over her shoulder to show off the diamond hair clip that locked everything in place.

"No, it won't happen again." She announced with authority as she cast her cane loose to stand by itself.

Lady Challis looked at her sister. "Why?"

"Petr is right, it was the first time and it will be the last. He won't react to human corpses that way again. Call it … my intuition."

A hard-metallic sound of a magazine being pushed into a gun cut through the conversation. Miray had reassembled her side arm; it was loaded and ready for action. She slipped it into her holster along with extra clips.

"It won't happen again," she looked at Gwendoline.

"I am good with that," said Miray. From her top pocket, one by one, she laid out the name tags they had collected from the dead guards.

"Elect-Si, you killed a guard before we entered the building; did you forget to take his name tag?"

"I got the tag." Elect-Si flipped the metal disk to Miray, who caught it effortlessly.

"The guard was female."

Miray half opened her mouth in surprise but said nothing. She rolled the tag over in her fingers and then studied the name.

"Female?"
"I know a vagina when I see one." Elect-Si said bluntly.

Miray looked sideways at Elect-Si.

"I have seen this name before… It is connected with the seminary where they castrate the young men." She gathered up the tags and put them in a shirt pocket.

"All the names, except the female guard, are on the roster of Cassius's little army."

" … and the contents of the container?"

"Two weeks ago, the container was reported washed overboard from a container ship in a storm. A storm we have not been able to locate."

For a long moment, there was silence. Elect-Si held out her glass for a servant to refill. She opened her mouth to speak but instead a large, long belch filled the room.

"Oh, while you ladies were comparing carcasses and genitals, I let myself in," said Wellington, smiling.

"Wellington. So good of you to announce yourself."

Wellington stood next to Lady Challis,

"Your daughter doesn't like. Will you protect me?"

Lady Challis smiled broadly.

"Elect-Si likes you very much. We are sorry we did not invite you … and your plate of food. Use that chair and side table." She gestured to a chair and table next to Petr.

Sitting down, Wellington placed his plate on the side table and turned to Petr,

"I guess all the cocks are sitting together… Do you have your balls? I do!" Then he turned back to his plate, which appeared to be steak, potatoes, and vegetables. He stabbed at the steak with his fork and cut off a piece and fed it into his mouth. As he set down his utensils, he pulled out some papers from the front of his Napoleonic era, a British army uniform jacket. He waved them vigorously at Elect-Si.

Slowly, she moved around to take them. She read them quickly and passed them to Miray. Miray read them and, one by one, dropped the pages on the table as she finished with them.

"Inventories. Ships Manifests. Transport carriers. Container leasing." She looked up at Wellington with a quizzical expression on her face.

Wellington was studying a baby carrot on his fork; some gravy dripped off it back on to the plate. The carrot disappeared into his mouth as he turned to look at Miray.

"Logistics Miray. We are dealing with a military regiment." He nodded knowingly at her.

"An army controlled by vampires' intent on having enough corpses to harvest organs and blood from to satisfy the need of their type and make a profit. It is also a farming collective. The small war they started and are forcing to continue allows them to harvest more. The problem is…" He paused to slice off another piece of steak and feed it into his mouth. They all had to wait for the rest of the sentence until he swallowed.

"Logistics always has an element of larceny, embezzlement, and fraud. They say an army marches on its stomach, but in reality, it marches on what is available to its stomach."

He looked down at his plate and stabbed at his steak.

"This meat is supposed to be cut from the thigh of an active 19-year-old human male. At least that is what the packaging said." He looked around the group.

"Chef and the doctor identified it as a cow, plain simple cattle meat. This gravy is supposed to be thickened with enriched 10% dried human brain. No. All corn. Just regular powdered gravy mix." Wellington looked around the room; all eyes were fixed on his plate.

Lady Challis turned back to her cards, a tarot deck and drew another card.

"The devil!" she held it up for all to see and then laid it down.

Wellington pushed the side table away and waved for a servant to take everything away.

"You are spending too much time fixated on Sophyra, Dorion, and that army Cassius has created for her." He paused and looked at Elect-Si and then Miray,

"When Sophyra became Pope, I thought we all agreed we would try and keep some degree of control over her. But we have none and we do not know the pressure points to exercise any sort of control."

Elect-Si reached down and picked up some of the papers, as she did, she looked across at Wellington and glared at him.

"Who told you to do this?" she said, waving the papers.

Wellington gestured to a servant to bring his desert.

"Miray. I don't have much to do around here. It seems I am left out of many things, which is something we need to talk about, but not now. I spent some time in logistics during the Napoleonic Wars. I started with what I know." He took his desert and held it so everyone could see the rich syrupy milk liquid in which floated small perfectly shaped balls.

"This is supposed to be ovaries from prepubescent girls with syrup enriched with semen from boys of the same age." He spooned one of the balls into his mouth.

"Sticky rice, cooked to be stickier than normal. There is nothing human in the syrup." He continued eating watched by everyone until he dropped his spoon in the empty bowl.

Elect-Si moved to a chair a short distance from where Miray sat and stared at him.

"With all the talk about harvesting humans, I decided to try some of the pre-packaged products. Burkhardt had chef order them for me. That is when we discovered the ruse. Let's face it, only the upper echelon of their kind, the Sophyra of this world, have will regularly eaten human meat and can tell the difference by taste." He stood up and patted his stomach.

"Back to work. Six freezer containers were shipped from the war last night, all supposedly full of human caresses."

Miray looked up at Elect-Si.

"We had to know; he was the best able to ferret it out."

Elect-Si stared at the papers; her eyes didn't focus on them. At the corner of her vision, she saw a neat pair of running shoes and pressed khaki pants. Her gaze moved up until she met familiar dark eyes. Her guide.

"Something complex, something dangerous is now in motion, spawned by the plan and your attention is elsewhere…" He half turned from where he sat and looked at Lady Challis still dealing cards for a Tarot reading.

"Your mother was attentive to her plan to create a female pope and that plan took over a millennium. Then someone took her goal, her plan, away from her. Do you think she stopped planning? No!" He slapped his knee.

"You became her plan."

"I made a mistake."

"Over a millennium, many mistakes happened; your mother moved on from each and every one of them. A mistake is an opportunity to learn, adapt, and change direction if needed." He pointed at the papers.

"There is information that can be useful." He stood up and looked at Lady Challis still dealing with her reading.

"Spend some time with your mother. You would both enjoy it."

For a moment, Elect-Si felt unsteady as her guide faded away and she was left with a room in silence, and unsure of why she was standing. As her mind steadied, she focused, she slid the papers neatly on the table.

"Miray, you did the right thing. Thank you."

9.   Altansarnai

Elect-Si rolled over and stretched in a way she did when she came home from a long flight to the Himalayas. Then she opened her eyes and looked out of the big doors on to the balcony and the riot of colourful flowers and glowing cloudless sky. In the bathroom, she heard her mother turn on the shower and start humming as she usually did when she was bathing.

It had been a good night, surprising in its hunger and intensity in their ability to give and receive love.

Her mother came from the bathroom, the shower still running for Elect-Si, just as her mother had done when her daughter first became a vampire. For some reason, she had always loved the heavy steam a hot shower could create. Now in northern India, it seemed the crisp cleanness of a cool or cold shower did the same for her.

Lady Challis moved barefoot across the floor in a thick colourful robe, her wet hair dripping small pools of water on to the floor behind her.

"Baby, the shower is perfect. Then check your tablet. Something interesting came in."

Elect-Si sat in the large chair, her legs curled up under her, not exactly a Lotus position, a loose cross of the legs, and maybe even a hug of her knees to her chest was more her style. They all helped send her mind into the calm clear space. Sometimes her guide would join her there, clarifying, and teaching. Always patient.

Next to him, for the first time, sat a girl, maybe 13 years old. She wore the distinctive, traditional clothing of women from the High Himalayas. Her wrists sat limply on her knees; her legs crossed. Suddenly, Elect-Si realized this was a lesson, not a meditation. She must observe, she must witness and understand the lesson. This may not be a new guide; it may be a teacher. So young!

"Altansarnai is not young, she has lived countless lives, so many even I cannot count them." Whispered her guide.

"Altansarnai means golden rose." He was not looking at her as he usually did when he spoke to her.

"She has been a white shaman all of her life. Unlike you, there is no scent of darkness in her. To draw the Ying and Yang of Altansarnai's soul would be to draw a white disk, like the sun at midday."

Elect-Si waited; there would be more to the scene. So far, there has been no lesson she could detect.

From the darkness, a large snake appeared, dark-coloured almost black. It was huge, like the ones in the videos she had seen of snakes in the Amazon. Forty feet long, maybe more, a massive girth and a heavy head with a wide mouth that can be made bigger by dislocating the jaw for easy swallowing. The forked tongue swept the air. The head followed the scent trails in the air that the tongue detected. Eyes seemed to shimmer, the vertical slit in them flexed open and closed like some mad lens.

The snake focused its attention on Altansarnai; it moved closer and coiled itself to give the head more height so it could look down on the girl.

Elect-Si knew that snakes hissed and could make sounds, but like all lessons her guide had given her, this one too was silent. Sounds he had explained one time could be distracting. There must be no distraction from what is to be learned. Elect-Si felt something welling up in her. There was unfocused concern for Altansarnai and the danger the malevolent snake threatened her with. Instinctively, Elect-Si looked around for a weapon. Slightly to the right of her hand, she found a rock. Oddly, it was perfectly shaped for her grip and came to a point. It might be flint, a flint tool. The point showed it had been worked by men chipping away at it. She realized it was sharper and deadlier than she first realized.

The snake made a lunge at Altansarnai, its jaws wide, saliva dripping off rows of evil yellow and blackened teeth. Elect-Si rocked back and forth slightly from where she sat; the snake's head moved like a bullet but missed. She blinked.

Yes, she knew snakes, like all predators, do not always get their prey every time they do miss their strike. The weight of the head carried it almost to the ground before the body convulsed and pulled it back to the striking position.

Altansarnai seemed unmoved, unconcerned.

The snake struck again and again but for some reason missed Altansarnai each time. Its body straightened as a shower of dirt fell from its nose.
Elect-Si tightened her grip on the rock. It was all she had but her intention was clear. The snake would not be allowed to strike again. From her position, her legs unfurled, and she was moving blindingly quickly and silently towards the back of the snake's body. She leaped and found her legs suddenly gripping the snake like a horse when she rode bareback. Her left hand, like a claw, dug into the scales on the back of the head, and gave her a grip that like a fisherman's hook, and which kept her attached to the great head.

She brought the rock down into one of the eyes and fluid gushed from it; the tongue swept up towards her but could not reach her. The animal started to gyrate as the coils supporting the snake's head now changed to help capture whatever it was on the back of its head.

Elect-Si knew she had to kill it quickly; she had used her advantage of surprise and violence; now she must do the deed before it could seize the advantage.

Elect-Si brought the rock point down hard on the bony skull. The sharpness of the flint cut through the scales surprisingly well, but the point skated off the bone underneath. She pulled her hand out from the gash in the scales. It was both covered in blood.

Fuck! How am I going to get through that hard bone into the brain? She readied for another strike but stopped. Inside her a white glow started to form; it felt as if it had been drawn up from the depths, shedding white light all the way, in the centre was a perfectly round shaped ball of blackness. Elect-Si grunted. She did not need an image of the white part of her Ying and Yang right now but the brightness of the image and the black ball in it seemed to draw her attention deeper and deeper. She breathed deeply, once, twice, and with the image blotting out even the massive snake head, she placed the blackness at the tip of the rock and drove it down with all the energy of the pure white energy.

She could feel bone cracking and splitting. Her fingers slammed against the skull bone, forcing her to let go of the rock, but as her fingers lost their grip, she could tell the rock had speed and force all of its own. It disappeared inside the skull into the brain with surprising energy. Her mind continued to push the rock even if she could not feel it.

Suddenly the ground slapped her hard on the back; the air in her lungs was burst from her mouth in a blast that made her lips hurt. She gasped to breathe, her lungs burned and her chest ached with the effort of expanding her lungs. Her mind struggled to comprehend what had happened.

All was blackness, then she realized her eyes were closed and she slowly opened them. She looked into the inscrutable eyes of Altansarnai.

"Stand. Stand! See what you have vanquished!"

Altansarnai stood up straight and held out her hand pointing to something Elect-Si could not see.

Elect-Si struggled to sit up and then stood. Several steps away, where the snake had been, lay the body of an old man, a large flint rock buried in the top of his head. Black blood was splattered all around in a large pool. His mouth open, showing blackened teeth that appeared to have been filed to points protruded from between his lips. She felt Altansarnai's hand slip into hers and guide her around the body.

"I saw a huge snake, not an old man." Protested Elect-Si looking from Altansarnai to her guide and back.

"I saw a snake as well; when it lunged at me, I deflected the head but I could feel the breath." Altansarnai paused,

"That is not an old man as you think of him. He was a great black shaman, someone who lived with and honoured the malevolent spirits. He was a caster of spells, someone who hurt, and killed, tortured, and mutilated with the help of black spirits from the Underworld. He was old when I first lived and became a white shaman."

"As I gathered my benevolent spirits around me. I learned that he was to be feared and should not be confronted. I was brave and young and confronted him and for doing so, I experienced pain and torment for the rest of that life. So much I cannot describe." Altansarnai looked at Elect-Si. And she sighed a sigh that seemed to pass through her body.

"He tormented me in each of my subsequent lives…" her voice trailed off.

"I suffered over and over but so many others have suffered even more because of him."

"As immortal as you are, what has gone before is unknown to you, only now, in this life, and the future is what your immortality will understand." Altansarnai held Elect-Si's hand more firmly as she turned to Elect-Si's guide.

"You are right."

Abruptly, Altansarnai turned and with her free hand slapped Elect-Si hard on the chest where her heart was.

"On the physical plane, shamans wear a toli and a mirror over their heart. A demon or a black shaman will see their own image in the toli when they attack and recoil away in fear. Now, open your shirt."

Elect-Si slowly unbuttoned her shirt and looked at the place over her heart. A Ying and Yang symbol, like a tattoo, but more than ink. A pearly white light from all that is white shone out and all that is black from a time before the universe was born pulsed.

"From the start of the universe! The essential whiteness and the essential blackness. Pure. Life had not started; nothing has tainted them. Anyone who confronts you will not understand how you can each at the same time." She let go of Elect-Si's hand.

"The black spirits, the black shamans, and all that are malevolent fear you because you hold a blackness they cannot comprehend. It is so much more than they are. The white shaman, the benevolent white spirits, honour you because you have a purity they venerate and respect."

"I am a white shaman, that is my oath, that is my nature, I am bound by my vow to the benevolent side." Elect-Si looked hard into Altansarnai's eyes.

"The blackness in me, the vampire, gives me the strength to destroy black spirits." Elect-Si looked over at the body, "and black shaman's too."

Altansarnai tilted her head to one side for a moment.

"Think of this. When you found you could not break through the skull with just the whiteness in you. You tipped the rock with your blackness and used the whiteness again to drive it down and pierce the bone easily." She breathed deeply.

"Thank you for removing my pain … for the healing you have given me." Altansarnai bowed, as she did, she faded away.

Elect-Si looked again towards the old shaman's body and watched as it too, slowly disappeared. She looked down at her chest; the Ying and Yang symbol was gone.

"It's left me!" she blurted out.

"No. Toli, such as shamans, wear on their costumes in the physical world are pieces of metal polished to be a mirror. They are to protect the heart from evil and malevolent spirits and shamans. Yours is wrapped all around, over and through your heart. Your heart is completely protected." He paused.

"I said there was doubt about you in the realms of the white and black spirts and among all shamans too. That is gone; it is clear now. You must accept your uniqueness. White and black spirits have fought since the start of time." He looked at the floor for a moment.

"You are both and separate; that is what Altansarnai said, and you have immortality. Such a unique being could bring peace, such as has never been seen."

"So, this was a lesson?" queried Elect-Si.

"A test."

"If I had failed?"

"The black shaman would have taken another piece of Altansarnai's soul and kept it to torture and mutilate it until the end of time."

"She was prepared to do that, to find out if what I say is true?"

"Yes."

"Her pain? Gone? Is she healed? Is there more I can do?

"Nothing else is needed of you; you have healed her from him by killing him."

He paused and looked at her for a long time in silence…

"You do such bewildering things…" He gestured to where the Black Shaman had lain.

"The whiteness of your shamanism allows you to embrace your blackness, and in so doing, you use blackness to kill. No one ever considered he could be killed. But above all, you are so … unexpected."

"It sounds as if you had dealings with him … how can I be unexpected?"

Her guide rubbed his eyes as if he were clearing them of old grime.

"Dealings? No, not me. But I know those who have. This has taken pain from so many. Altansarnai taught and helped me guide souls and spirits, and to never fear." He took several steps closer.

"The Ying and Yang has always been a metaphor for good and evil… I am sure you know the words … the white and black are complementary rather than opposing energies, but you literally are the Ying and Yang of existence in the physical and spiritual realms. You are each, and one." He looked into her eyes as if he were searching for something.

"I'm not sure what you are looking for, I am just me."

"That is what is so unexpected. Go Elect-Si, your breakfast is getting cold."
Elect-Si blinked and looked at her hands; they cradled a big mug of coffee; only a few wisps of steam came from it as it cooled. She waved to a servant to bring a new mug as hot as they could provide. She smiled across the table at her mother. Nut Gwendoline's eyes blazed with something… admiration!

10.   Potting Plants

The old man stood up, pushing the stool back so he could admire his work.

"Completely undetectable," he murmured. On the bench, between the small potted plants lay the focus of his attention and admiration. Two well-made wooden pegs about three inches long connected in the middle by unusually strong monofilament. He picked it up, allowing the monofilament to pass between his second and third fingers. The filament was long enough he mused to allow Phaedra to easily wrap it around the neck of someone … he would not say who, but he knew who he wanted it to be. Pulling the pegs tight behind the neck would garotte the victim. He had abraded the monofilament so the roughness provided a cutting edge if Phaedra needed to see through the victims' neck to the spine.

For a moment, he stood transfixed by what he had made. His mind tumbled back centuries to the Inquisition. It had been on a small hill top outside of Cadiz. He had watched disgusted and fascinated as a Catholic priest placed an iron collar around the neck of a condemned English sailor. Slowly the priest tightened the collar and continued tightening until death relieved the sailor of his heretical Protestant beliefs.

The bishop next to him immediately started berating the priest. Death was too fast; the condemned was to see the folly of their heretical religion as life slowly ebbed from them. They were to know what it was to struggle without hope; heresy could never bring any good to the condemned. The dying was to look at the Catholic priest administering their strangulation and know who was acting as the hand of God; it was to be slow and take time.

Injury to the spinal column at the base of the brain had killed the sailor too quickly. The priest must learn how to use the contraption so that this does not shorten the time it takes to die.

He prodded the fat old bishop in the belly with his shepherd's crook and berated him. Finally, the bishop resettled his cloak and turned to walk to his carriage; he had to be at the seminary in the centre of the city by midday.

Slowly, he wrapped the garotte up and placed it in the corner of the envelope containing the herbs that prevented Phaedra from getting pregnant.

As he finished putting the envelope in his large side pocket, his mind continued to roll around the image of the Bishop.

This time, the Bishop was lying on the ground, screaming, and writhing, his rich ornate cloak being ground into the dirt and his ceremonial headdress kicked around like an inflated pigs' bladder by some children.

The bishop had supervised the garrotting of a vampire, a few days before. It had taken over twenty minutes for the vampire to die, as the bishop had the garotte tightened and loosened over and over again.

Now the Bishop lay on the floor, his knees smashed by a blacksmith's hammer. Quickly he stooped down and put the garotte around Bishop's neck.

The old man frowned as he straightened his jacket and prepared to leave to meet Phaedra. The garrotting of the Bishop had been too quick, but it had satisfied the community, and that was the main thing.

11.   Banjhakri

Amunet walked barefoot through the rich green grass seemingly oblivious to the Banjhakri watching her lithe body move under the simple silk dress.

"You can't fuck her. You know that?" said Elect-Si.

"Yes, I know, she is a Primordial Goddess. The Hidden One." His words paused for a long moment.

"The air, she is the goddess of air and what is invisible. She holds the souls of the dead until she is ready to be reborn … there are some souls she still holds and they scream … scream like a tree being burned while it is still planted in the ground." He turned to look at Elect-Si.

"I am glad you are here. I am glad your heart is protected." He reached out as if trying to slip his hand under Elect-Si's blouse but she pushed his hand away.

"My guide said I will be protected forever and that it is a powerful protection."

"More than powerful," he looked back at Amunet, "like her, primordial. Nothing can be greater. The darkness and the light of the universe before life started. But now you have that, what do you need with me, a simple man of the forest?"

"You taught me, you trained me. I want to make sure you are protected."

"You fear for me? That is nice, thank you. If you worry that black spirits will come for me … that has already happened, they came to make me pay for training you." He looked at her deeply.

"But I dealt with them. They are gone."

"Is your mate safe?"

"My mate … she is safe."

"Truth, I demand truth!"

The Banjhakri fidgeted.

"Truth!"

"She was injured, but she has healed now. She has been cleansed of any darkness."

"Truth!"

The Banjhakri sighed deeply.

"A part of her soul was taken to the underworld."

Elect-Si started to open her mouth but Amunet's slender finger crossed it, and stopped her.

"I know where the fragment is. I will show you."

Abruptly to her right, Elect-Si's guide appeared.

"Have you come to watch?"

"Maybe, yes, or no… You will be doing this by yourself…"

"Unless I need help?"

"Yes, I am your guide and guides; well, they show the way and they advise. You will see things you have not encountered before. Use that excellent mind of yours; do not rely on your invincibility."

"Is that all?" asked Amunet.

Elect-Si's guide looked at her intently for a long moment. It was evident he was not used to a different spirit, being able to see him and interact with him. He shrugged,

"You know the underworld as well as anyone; you know what she will encounter."

12.   The Underworld

Amunet slipped her hand into Elect-Si' and like the start of a movie, she found herself by the side of a wide lake, with thick reeds along its banks. A gentle breeze was blowing across the lake, causing the surface to ripple. The air smelled fresh, moist and of growing things. The sky was dark and the stars were out, a crescent moon hung in the sky. Across the water, an old worn boat dock extended from the shore; a small camp fire flickered to one side.

Elect-Si walked to the top of a small mound. The grass felt wet under her feet, the night's dew had already formed and was trickling down the blades into the ground. She felt something in her hand; she looked down; it was her cane. Its tip floated above the ground, as always, but now it seemed to be forceful and something she could lean on.

"You said you know where the soul fragment is."

"I do, but I also want to show you the underworld, the world that I know so well."

"Underworld, I have always thought of it being black and nasty; this is not so bad. Is it always like this?

"Just like the middle world, there is day and night. Plants need sunlight for photosynthesis just the same."

Elect-Si whirled around at the sound of a rustling sound behind her.

"Is this a family outing?" she said to her guide.
"I am your guide; I go everywhere with you. Amunet is a special guide; she is here teaching you something."

"I am here to recover the soul fragment; this is like a shaman's soul journey."

"And?"

"The dark spirit that took it will pay for taking it." Elect-Si's jaw took on a firm, hard line.

"Amunet, can you tell me, show me, give me a clue?"

A breeze started to ruffle the tops of the tallest trees and started to move the reeds around. The ripples on the water became deeper and covered the lake from end to end. Abruptly, Amunet clapped her hands. The breeze suddenly stopped, and everything became quiet. The lake surface became like a mirror perfectly reflecting the sky and moon, which had risen higher and was shedding more light on the landscape and the dock.

"Are we going to stand here all night?" Amunet asked.

"You were going to show me where the sprit is and the soul fragment, I am waiting for you."

"What did your guide say?"

"Really! You're asking that?" Elect-Si turned and looked at her guide but he shrugged his shoulders. Still looking at her guide, she slowly said…

"I have to use my excellent mind."

She turned to look across the lake at the campfire. There must be something important here. She turned around slowly, studying the trees, which remained still, like the water and the rushes all were calm.

"The campfire. There is no one around it; no smell of smoke and no smoke in the air. We should be over there."

Amunet held out her hand for Elect-Si. But Elect-Si shrugged,

"We can walk around."

Amunet gripped Elect-Si's wrist,

"You may have all night, I do not. Spread those blue wings princess; we are flying across."

Elect-Si stared at the fire; it was yellow and red, with some odd tinges of pure blue. It seemed to be burning a few inches above the grass, which was not consumed by the flames. There was no wood in the fire; there were just flames appearing out of thin air. For some reason, she held out her cane in the direction of the fire and watched, surprised as the fire shied away from the cane, as if it were frightened of it.

"I guess the fire is not a fire in the real sense," she said and stooped down to grasp one of the tongues of flame.

As she did so, the fire drew in on itself and something blue and glowing fell on to the ground. As the flames disappeared, a looming black shape came into existence by the fire. It was several inches taller than Elect-Si, dressed in a long cloak and large hood falling over its head. In its hand, it held a scythe,

"The grim reaper, is that the best you can do?" She muttered.

For a moment the figure stood transfixed by the words and slowly changed into a large snake, smaller in size than the one Elect-Si had killed but it immediately started to move towards her, hissing and its wide mouth opening and closing. Elect-Si waited for it to draw closer,

"I have killed a black shaman masquerading as a large snake."

The snake's head drew closer and closer and stopped feet from Elect-Si, its eyes apparently fixated on the rising and falling of her breasts, its mouth opened and fangs dripping poison extended. At the last few feet, it turned back and changed into a shabbily dressed black shaman, his eyes glittered intently. He reached out to take a piece of her heart, her soul, with his dirty grubby hands and fingers ending in broken and blackened nails. In the last moment, she could see his face register shock, pain, and horror.

He recoiled and stepped back. He pulled the worn clothes over his frame as if they were a shield.

"Such blackness … beyond death." Spittle drooled at the corners of his mouth.

"Such whiteness…" responded Elect-Si.

The old man scowled and waved his hands in the air at the word; the thought of whiteness was abhorrent to him.

In his throat, the sound of mucus and phlegm gathered and erupted from his mouth in a long stream in her direction. Abruptly her cane left her hand and hovered in front of the odious black stream, the crystal glowing brightly. The spirit in the cane deflected the stream of fluid, which landed short and to one side. His eyes narrowed as he stared at the cane.

"Why do you bother me? I was a fire and I enjoyed it. The heat warms these old bones and the soul of that Banjhakrini, such great fuel, such great fuel…" his voice trailed off into a cough that shook his entire body. His lips parted in a contorted grin, his black teeth, dull, pitted, and pointed, lined his lips and were licked by a horribly black tongue.

"I came for that soul fragment, and I came to punish you for taking it."

"You cannot punish me. You may have killed a black shaman, one who was beloved of all of us here. That happened in the Lower World, this," he waved his arm to indicate all around him.

"This is the Underworld; you cannot kill me here. I am too powerful."

Elect-Si looked around, being careful not to lose sight of the black spirit as she did. Dim, dark shapes were starting to appear, all indistinct, taking on no real form. The water in the lake seemed to be filled with small watery fountains as if something under the surface was pushing upward to release itself. Water splashed at the end of the dock.

"Your Toli is so, so powerful, but I will find your weakness. I will show it to the others…" he looked around his hands fidgeting in the air indicting the other spirits present,

Elect-Si stared at him. Her wings were not fully folded and hidden away; they were open just enough to give a quick violent burst of speed and she would have him. She shot forward at a speed that surprised even her.

The dark spirit moved to one side but her cane smashed its golden tip into his forehead, making him reel back with a loud scream into her path. Her right hand trailed slightly beneath her on that side. The first two fingers slammed into the right eye and the third and fourth fingers into the left. She gripped tightly, the orbs broke open, spilling their fluid into the air and now her hand held his head by her fingers in his empty eye sockets. Her wings abruptly extended and gave a powerful best to get them airborne.

Elect-Si circled for a moment then dove down to the ground where Amunet and her guide stood. A moment before she landed, she placed her feet behind his knees and drove them into the ground. Snapping them like twigs. The dark spirit screamed and flailed his arms in vain. She brought her wings in a little tighter so the wing claws could brutally stab into the spirits' shoulders. She smashed each shoulder joint in turn.

Elect-Si reached down and grasped one of his flailing arms; she pulled it backward and upward with a strength and dexterity she had not seen in herself before. She could sense the tearing of sinews and tendons. Strangely, the skin started to separate.

For a moment, she was transfixed by the memory of her father, when she was still a young girl. It was Christmas; they were seated around the table. He was carving Turkey. To separate the drum sticks as he called them, he simply tore them from the carcass and the crispy cooked skin broke open as the joint appeared. She watched the skin break open as she twisted and pulled.

Thick black blood oozed from the open socket, and dripped from the arm. She studied it for a moment and dropped it on the ground. She tore the other arm off and dropped it beside the other.

More screaming and wailing like a banshee erupted from his mouth and thicker black blood started to pour out of his other socket, burning the grass.

She pushed the spirit prone on the ground and stood on its back. She turned and used her wing claws to smash the hip joints and pulled a broken leg backward until she had ripped it from his torso. She did the same with the other leg.
She inserted her fingers back into his bloody eye sockets. She pulled back and up; his mouth opened and like a powerful predator, a wing claw broke through the teeth and hooked his tongue. She ripped it from his mouth. She looked down at the body parts.

"If you can create fire, so can I." Elect-Si looked at her guide with a quizzical expression on her face. As if, asking how do I create fire.

Elect-Si put her hands together and started to rub. A powerful, astonishingly bright pure light appeared that instantly made her hands appear translucent. She slowly parted her hands and a column of concentrated white flame grew and grew until it lit the thin clouds high above as far as she could see in all directions.

All around her, she was aware of the other dark spirts, under the water, in the soil, all moving away from the column of light and the pureness it gave. After admiring the whiteness of the column of fire, she fed the body parts, one by one, into it. They disappeared in a brief shower of sparks and odd black feathery flames.

At the end, her guide indicated she should clap her hands, which she did and the column of fire was gone. Slowly the land and the water went back to the dim light of the moon.

Elect-Si stood in silence for what seemed like several minutes. While the column of fire had lit the ground all around, her sharp vampire eyes had spotted a grove of Yew saplings and their parent tree.
Her wings beat and, and she took off in the direction of the trees. One by one she walked through the grove, inspecting each in turn. When she found one, she admired and knew she could do the job she would assign it. She stopped and held the sapling's trunk and gently whispered and incantation. Tree by tree, the trees came loose, their strong roots giving up their hold in their soil.

As she landed at the torso of the black spirit, she saw the armless and legless shape squirming like a magot. She stepped forward and placed a stiletto on its spine and moved it to find a vertebra. She pressed down and the sound of bone cracking was sharp and telling. She moved her heel to another vertebra and split that one.

Finally, she brought a wing claw down on to the pelvis and broke it in two. Then she ripped the remnants of clothing from the immobile shape at her feet.

She drove one sapling through each shoulder into the ground and one through each of his broken hips. Sapling by sapling, she whispered an invocation. Visibly, the roots spread over and through the torso into the ground. The body moved as the Yew saplings strengthened their hold on it. One by one, Elect-Si took a leaf from each tree.

As she stood back from the broken black shaman, her hand floated for a moment in still air, she felt the handle of her cane fill her palm and she instinctively gripped it.

"So, here is the deal." She looked around briefly at the other shapes that had reappeared.

"A soul fragment was taken by this black shaman from the mate of a Banjhakri who is close to me. I am taking it back and I am punishing him." She kicked the ribs of the spirit and pressed her stiletto into the spine, snapping another vertebra.

"I took out and burned his tongue so he cannot cast spells. I ripped off his arms and burned them so he cannot conjure spells and do evil by gesture. I took his legs so he cannot walk to get help. He is blind so he cannot see what or who is around him." She stooped and jabbed her fingers into his ears.

"He is deaf." She turned a full circle and pointed her cane at every deformity in the land and water.

"These Yew trees will shed poison fruit, needles, and their bark on him." She admired the saplings for a long moment.

"I have given an invocation to each tree. They will grow big, strong, and powerful. They will never die; they cannot be cut down, burned, or starved of what they need to grow. They are resistant to spells, and to all evil." She held up a leaf she had taken from each tree.

"I will know, and will come back if any of you find a way to harm a tree and you will meet a similar fate." She picked up the soul fragment she had come to retrieve. She pointed at the spirit lying staked out on the ground.

"This is an eternal punishment, a warning never to touch anything, or anyone close to me."
She turned to Amunet, who seemed a little surprised, but admiring.

"Let's get the fuck out of here."

13.   A judgment

Elect-Si ran her fingers along the edge of the table and smoothed out the crisp white cotton table cloth with its rich satin embroidery. The sun was just an hour past sunrise; the reflecting lake to her left was like glass; it held a shimmering copy of the palace and the growing brightness of the sun in its high cirrus clouds.

Servants stood ready at the breakfast carts lined up around the table like a ring of pioneer wagons protecting it. A large ornate sun shade completely shielded the table; its embroidered tassels hanging limply in the still air. To her right, her cane stood upright, its gold tip a few inches from the ground.

"Sorry I am late..." murmured Burkhardt as he walked briskly up to the table and sat down. He nodded to the servants to start serving breakfast.

"Mother is very disappointed in you," said Elect-Si as she looked at her French style scrambled eggs, bacon, and dark rye toast dripping with melted butter. She sprinkled sea salt, cracked black pepper, and a liberal dusting of dried blood flakes over the eggs and watched the flakes mop up moisture from the eggs and turn back to delicious tasty globules of blood. Those red pearls were so much tastier than ketchup!

She looked up at Burkhardt. Today was his day of reduced duties and he did not have a dress shirt on, a simple loose Indian-style long white cotton shirt over black baggy pants. He was not wearing shoes. His hair was a little less kempt than normal and it appeared he had not shaved. He reached for a glass of his favourite mix, orange juice, and swirled into it, O negative blood. He seemed to be looking into the glass in a contemplative mood ... as well he might.

"Disappointed! Is that all, I thought our relationship warranted more than disappointment?"

"Burkhardt, you were fucking two maids, and both are pregnant. All I can say is that it is a good thing both are our kind," said Elect-Si as she started to eat.

"You have duties to the lady of the house; keeping her happy and satisfied is one of them."

There was a long pause before Burkhardt replied. He had deliberately filled his mouth to give him time to consider his reply. He looked past Elect-Si, his eyes fixed on a person walking over to the table.

The figure bushed past Elect-Si, a slender hand appeared and took some bacon from Elect-Si's plate. A servant hurried to set a place and prepare the setting for the visitor.

Gwendoline sat down at an angle to Burkhardt; she was looking directly at Elect-Si, a grin spreading across her lips. She winked at Elect-Si.

"I heard about your little soiree into the Underworld last night. You must invite me next time; I want to see you in action. According to Amunet, you are quite something. So fast … so brutal and a large dose of cruelty." She paused as she studied Elect-Si.

"I can sense your Toli, which is something very, very different."

"Could I come too?" Asked Burkhardt, grasping at a possible change of subject to away the displeasure Lady Challis had with her head butler.

Gwendoline looked from Elect-Si to Burkhardt and straightened her seating position as she chewed on the bacon. As she did, a breakfast plate was set before her with a glass of blood.

"Mother is very disappointed in Burkhardt," said Elect-Si.

"I would think so, two maids knocked up, what were you doing sleeping with both of them at the same time?"

"In the same bed at the same time," interrupted Elect-Si.

Burkhardt looked crestfallen that the details of his sexual preferences were known so clearly. If she knew, so would Lady Challis.

"I must meet with your mother today. I guess…. I guess judgment has to be passed?" He asked.

Elect-Si picked up two strands of bacon and sniffed at them and then cautiously bit into each in turn and chewed slowly to get the full taste and flavour of the cooked meat.

"I am to pass judgment." Said Elect-Si turning back to her eggs and started loading them on to her toast.

Gwendoline chuckled.

"Burkhardt, you are so fucked! Well, that is what you have been doing too much. Elect-Si, we should send him to that seminary, where they castrate young humans for Dorion's army and have Reverend Mother Phaedra cut them off. At least he won't get any more maids pregnant."

"She is a Reverend Mother now?"

"Oh, that is what I call her. Dorion persuaded Pope Sophyra to make Phaedra Superior General of a new religious order and institution to bring formality to what she is doing. The institution will sanctify the right to both harvest and castrate humans. The seminary is pretty empty now; all the regular religious studies and teaching have moved out. They can't stand Phaedra."

"No, please. Elect-Si, I like my balls…"

"That is a very good idea … it aligns with the traditional punishment in a way." Elect-Si put down the bacon and asked a servant for a fresh serving and pointed at some, which was slightly less crispy.

"Did you not like that bacon?" asked Burkhardt.

"It's made of humans, isn't it? The bacon that is slightly lighter and not as crispy," interrupted Gwendoline.

Burkhardt looked from Elect-Si to Gwendoline and then down at his plate. Without realizing it, he had pushed the lighter and less crispy bacon to one side and was not eating it.

"Yes. Dorion is marketing it for people who cannot eat pig meat. I err, don't like it much either." He picked up his glass of blood and juice and sipped at it slowly, looking over the rim at Elect-Si.

"Please, pass judgment now … so I may go and carry it out."

Gwendoline dabbed at the corner of her lips with her napkin and looked at Elect-Si.

"I vote we send Burkhardt to Phaedra and let her have her way with him."

"Burkhardt, you know what the traditional punishment is … don't you?" Asked Elect-Si

Burkhardt suddenly seemed to lose energy and slumped in his chair.

"Yes, of course." He sighed heavily;

"Mary and Gemma came to me the night they found out all naked, and beautiful and wonderful and soft, and fuckable. They wanted to tell me together. They … they have no idea of the meaning. Each was so proud to be carrying my baby. No idea of tradition. Not a thought. My god, I wanted to do them so badly, but now."
"Did you tell them?"

"No, I could not bear the thought of doing so."

"Tell me what you understand of the traditional judgment?"

"Elect-Si, get on with it, stop dragging this out!" Blurted Gwendoline.

Burkhardt pushed his breakfast plate away.

"I…" he stammered, "I am to tie each of them up. I am to cut out the fetus while they are alive, then cut their throats and drink from their necks. I have to make sure the fetus is dead. I burn everything about them on a rubbish pile, not a pyre. They are to have no honours. I am never to speak of them again."

He looked at Elect-Si, "Did I miss anything?"

Elect-Si licked her fingers from the butter on her toast,

"You forgot why you are doing this. No one cares if a maid gets pregnant. Why is this important?"

"Why…" repeated Burkhardt.

"Why I am doing this? It is because if Lady Challis, head of our lineage, is to have a child, it is to be either another vampire of her equal, or by her chief servant." Slowly Burkhardt picked up his breakfast knife and looked at it.

Elect-Si sipped at her coffee.

"Exactly. I am glad you understand." Her eyes locked on Burkhardt, she sipped her coffee again.

"Then listen to my judgment. Do you swear an oath to follow it?"

Burkhardt's eyes disengaged from Elect-Si's; he looked down at his plate.

"Yes, I swear an oath to follow your guidance, and to carry out your blessed judgment. Thank you. I honour you."

"Mary and Emma are to live with you. They are to deliver their babies normally, and you will be a father to the babies. You are to be married to both women until they die … naturally."

Burkhardt closed his eyes and dropped the knife back on his plate.

"How can I thank you?"

"You can't, not yet anyway. I will let you know when I need you to do something for me. Now go and service those women."

Burkhardt slowly got up.

"When you need that something … ask. I will be therefore you." He straightened himself and slowly walked away.

Gwendoline looked curiously at Elect-Si.

"I don't understand you. What you did last night and what you did just now." She looked quizzically into Elect-Si's eyes.

"You know, it is a tradition that, on a soul retrieval, you bargain and negotiate with the dark spirit that took it?"

"He did not take the soul fragment to negotiate; it was to draw me to the Underworld and try and take a fragment of my soul. He knew of the Black Shaman I killed earlier but not the Toli I have."

"Yes, that Toli. It vibrates at a frequency I can just sense it is so high. But then again, I have not been to that time when the universe had not been created to experience the absolute darkness and light of creation." She looked away in the direction Burkhardt had taken.

"Did Challis really give you the power of judgment?"

"Yes." Elect-Si paused; she sensed her own never-ending existence.

"No Matter how many heirs she has, or by whom, they can never inherit simply because there will never be a void for them to fill."

Gwendoline looked down at her plate and started to heap her eggs up on her toast.

"The only one who could inherit something is you, who, as humans say, bends the knee to Challis." She sighed,

"You could have given a traditional judgment and brought Burkhardt to his knees."

"Gwen, you are thinking of me as a vampire, all dripping evil, and darkness, like in the movies. You forget I am a white shaman; the whiteness in my Ying and Yang is balanced by my darkness. I am in balance. The dark spirit saw my blackness, Burkhardt and my whiteness."

"It will take some time. For now, I have difficulty understanding you." She looked past Elect-Si at the cane.

"That," She pointed.

"Is quite a cane, your shaman's staff I mean. It is enormously powerful in its own right and the spirits in it need treating with respect, even love. It is yours, and yours alone. Amunet said you used it as a weapon, an extension of yourself. It can also make decisions that will help you. I… I have never quite mastered that."

Elect-Si picked up a couple of pieces of pork bacon and placed them on Gwendoline's plate.

"Eat your pork; it seems from your plate that you don't like the human version either."

14.   Logistics

Phaedra smiled an artificial smile. Dorion could be so crude. So relentlessly crude. In front of her, Dorion was modelling a new habit she had designed for herself. It looked like a bad Halloween costume.

"Like?" asked Dorion, making a long slow twirl that showed the skirt had slits at the side to reveal her legs and the leather boots she was wearing.

The only thought in Phaedra's mind was the garotte woven into her own, much simpler habit. She could clearly see it wrapped tightly around Dorion's small neck, cutting through that pale white skin to the spine and spilling blood everywhere. It would be interesting to see if Dorion's blood was red, or black, as some rumours said.

"Perhaps the suspenders could be leather?" ventured Phaedra.

The image of Dorion dying by the garotte continued to float through her mind like a beautiful butterfly that looked so impossibly good it could not be real. But she knew it would be, and soon, the gardener had told her so.

Just a little longer and she would be able to catch that butterfly, kill it, and ascend to the head of the new institution, one seat away from Pope Sophyra. Then, she would catch another butterfly, Sophyra, and the plan for her to be on the Holy Seat would be complete.

"Oh, when I am in public, I lose the suspenders. They are decoration anyway."

Phaedra continued to unroll the large maps and sheets of paper on the old refectory table.

"Hmmm, the war is going well; it could be better if we extend it here; there will be more human casualties for us to collect." She tapped a city with one of her long nails.

Phaedra nodded but she found it difficult to be happy at the thought of the death and destruction such a simple tap of a nail on a map, thousands of miles away, could bring to a peaceful location.

"Make sure the city is sealed off before we start. I want a maximum cull." Dorion's eyes met Phaedra's.

"Maximum cull; is that understood?"

"Yes, maximum cull. That is understood."

Dorion pouted, and smiled.

"It is so much easier to work with you than Casius. Is he still fucking you?"

"Yes, nightly."

"When are you supposed to go to Alessandro for him to impregnate you?"

"Alessandro has passed away. It is said he died with a nun riding him." Phaedra lets a small, thin smile cross her lips.

"Now that is surprising … isn't it?" Dorion pushed the map away and pulled another large sheet towards her.

"Although he was old, he was fit and healthy."

"Sorry, I always get turned on by the thought of someone I want culled being … culled." Her gaze focused on Phaedra and she turned back to the papers on the table.

"Perhaps Alessandro's death was not from his exercise, as he called it?" Queried Phaedra.

Dorion did not answer; she was engrossed in the statistics on the paper she held. She looked up and out of the window; she was deep in thought.

"Are you in love with Casius? Would you cull him if I asked?" Question Dorion.

Phaedra looked out of the window, feigning interest in the view of the gardens. Then her eyes found her gardener far at the end, pruning the rose bushes. As he moved, she could see the stiffness in his arthritic legs; her heart ached to find some way to help him. Then her mind turned back to Dorion and she turned to look at her.

"I do not love him. He is a means to an end. If he is to be culled, I will enjoy doing it."

Without speaking, Dorion turned and walked to her desk. She unlocked a drawer with her finger print and took out a small pouch; she opened it as if checking the contents and then closed it. She walked back to Phaedra and laid it open on the table.

"The red file contains a heart-stopping drug. Put a few drops somewhere he likes to kiss and lick. Then start fucking him. He will be dead in a few minutes. The harder you ride him the quicker it will be. Before you start, take a few drops of the liquid in the other file that is the antidote. Take it directly on your tongue, in wine, water … whatever." Dorion closed the pouch and pushed it to Phaedra.

Phaedra reached for it and smiled.

"When? Any reason?"

"Not yet, I will send word." She looked at Phaedra as if weighing the need to give instructions.

"A few last things have to be cleared up. It is possible Casius may have been motivated to create this army of castrates by someone who does not have Pope Sophyra's best interests at heart. Let's leave it there." Dorion returned to look at the papers.

"Thank you. He will be dead the night you send word."

"When I send word, I want Casius dead as soon as possible. Is that understood?" the words were cold and brittle.
"Yes. Of course. I understand perfectly."

Slowly Dorion started to fold one of the large sheets of paper.

"Increase shipments of the rare earth minerals and diamonds, but especially uranium. Even if it means leaving bodies to rot on the battle field. We have too many dead humans all of a sudden." Dorion paused and suddenly threw the folded paper violently across the table.

"Do you know we are selling human meat to humans as fake pig products!" Her hands waved uncontrollably in the air.

"We had six containers arrive with war-damaged bodies yesterday. My butchers said it was not worth their time trying to retrieve anything saleable. The containers should have been pushed overboard." Dorion took a deep breath, which made her breasts rise suggestively.

"Take control of the next batch of your fighters. Get some control over the supply chain, and improve the quality of what we are receiving. I would rather have one container of usable bodies than six that are not. Understand?"

"Yes, of course.

"It is as Pope Sophyra wishes," snapped Dorion. For a moment there was a silence, so still Phaedra could hear the birds in the garden and the gardener putting away his tools.

"Well! What are you waiting for? Fuck off!" Snapped Dorion

15.   Manuel

Lady Challis leaned back into the deeply cushioned chair and stared out over the rooftops of the Alfama District of Old Town Lisbon. The sun was coming up, the sky was yellow, orange, and red, matching the clay roof tiles perfectly. The rich scent of flowers wafted over to her and she kicked off her shoes and folded her legs under her as she sank further into the deep cushions of the abundant wicker chair.

The sound of ships' horns echoed through the port as they navigated in and out, reminding her of the bustling activity here. It was just as lively back in the 15th century when she last visited. That was the golden age of the Portuguese Renaissance, when the voyages of discovery ignited the Portuguese colonial empire. So much energy and vitality filled the air! First, they explored the islands of the Azores, Madeira, and Cape Verde. Then, they discovered the route to India around the Cape of Good Hope and, of course, Brazil. No matter what the Spanish were up to, it seemed Portugal had enough to keep them busy. She couldn't help but smile, thinking about how small the world really was back then!

The Portuguese Renaissance created a plethora of poets, historians, critics, theologians, and moralists. She reached out and looked at her hand; she gently rubbed her thumb and forefingers together as if she were twirling the stem of a wine glass. The last time she had performed such a delicate act was when she and Prince Henry the Navigator had stayed up late talking politics and navigation. She sighed, such times were long past, not lost, just past. This house, the sun rose, was bringing them back. The prince's eyes sparkled when he talked about the plans for his Portuguese people and the new world. It was a rare occasion, if she were honest, that she came closest to revealing who and what she was. He was talking about land, soil, riches, spices, people, and animals that she had already seen.

The thirty-first century before Christ and Pharaoh Narmer was dead. His son by Queen Neithhotep, Hor-Aha had succeeded him. Lady Challis looked at her nails; she had seen it coming. She was not of royal blood and Narmer had married a member of the ancient royal line to secure the right of succession for any heir he had. Challis did not want to be part of another reign; Narmer's Egypt and the unification of the Upper and Lower kingdoms had been enough. Really. Enough. Where Narmer had been outward looking in trade and engagement in the region, Hor-Aha was focused on only the lush and fertile Nile Valley.

Pharaoh Narmer was one of a very select few humans she had loved, truly loved, deeply loved, admired and honoured. The Nile flooded the year her beloved died. A servant told her it was the tears she shed every day that event that had made the river overflow. All she could think of was leaving, starting anew, as she had done so very many times before.

Amunet felt her loss too; it seemed even the mighty Goddess knew hurt. She seduced Challis with stories of the world her winds blew over that no Egyptian or European had seen or dreamt of. It would be a challenge, she said, to fly to these places and spend time there. Amunet would help but Challis had to fly across a great sea. Something Challis had never done before. Adventure was calling. The new lands would take her breath away!

A maid appeared with a breakfast tray and started to busy herself setting the table. As she turned, she saw Lady Challis so beautifully relaxed and at peace in the large comfortable chair. The maid froze. This was a visitor she did not know had arrived, and whom she had ever seen before.

"Tell Manuel … tell him, Lady Challis is here, and set up another place. I will be staying for breakfast," smiled Lady Challis.

The maid stood rooted to the spot for a few more moments and then rushed inside the house.

Lady Challis looked back at the sun rise, the face of her beloved Narmer fixed in her mind. She brought two fingers to her lips and gently blew a kiss to the sunrise and Narmer's lips.

Her death, like all before, would be faked. An immortal who wants to die and move on to a new life always has to fake their death, even if they fervently, with all their heart, want to truly die. Lady Challis went down to the Nile under the pretext of helping with the rescue and feeding of dispossessed farmers from royal granaries. Crossing the Nile on a Felucca, Amunet would create a gust of wind that would capsize the boat. Lady Challis would be thrown into the water, and that would be the last anyone would see of her. She would be presumed drowned, and washed downstream, or eaten by crocodiles.

A year later, Challis sat on a ridge hugging her knees to her chest looking down on Machu Picchu, busy with worshippers, priests, and nobles dressed in a huge array of animal skins and brightly coloured feathers from jungle birds.

Amunet cast a sideways glance at Lady Challis. She stared out at the thermal currents of the valley. She waited and then sent a small oval rock skipping across the tops of the thermals like a child skipping stones across the surface of a lake. Finally, the rock lost its energy and fell into the deep, deep valley.

"I hope it doesn't hit anyone, or anything." Said Amunet quietly, then she turned around to stare at Lady Challis.

"Is Machu Picchu not enough?" she asked.

"You like skipping rocks across the tops of thermal currents, don't you?" Smiled Lady Challis.

"It's not fair, even I can't do that. You control the wind; you just make the thermals as hard as needed to get it to skip."

Amunet shrugged.

"So, what if I do, I can have fun with the thermals in the way human children skip rocks on water? You didn't answer the question. Has anything we have seen and done for the past year given you any joy?"

Lady Challis focused on two brightly plumed nobles on one of the large green grassy platforms.

"Look, I think they are going to fight."

"Don't change the subject!" Snapped Amunet

Lady Challis fell silent and the nobles appeared to have backed away from fighting. She hugged her knees a little more tightly.

"Yes, it has helped a lot. Thank you. I have never said that before. Thank You Amunet for caring and giving me this wonderful year."

"That continent, down under, you said it would be called Australia. My heart was lost there, so beautiful and the tribal people so gentle," she fell silent and looked around Machu Picchu one more time.

"But the other part of your heart is lying in a sarcophagus back in Egypt." Amunet turned to look where Lady Challis was gazing.

"You are an immortal vampire, Narmer was human. You never bit him; that would have at least given him a longer life for you two to be together."

"I know, I have thought about that over and over again. Should I have, should I not … well we know the answer to that. I wanted to be there at the moment of his passing, I wanted to see his soul leave his body and I wanted to see you receive him. Queen Kenthap would not allow me to be there. I had a right to be there and witness the last moment of his soul."

"To Kenthap, you were just a high-ranking female official who was fucking her husband. I am not surprised you were not allowed. That moment was for her and her family."

"Djer would have over ruled her if he had been older."

"There is another problem. You got on too well with Narmer's son. He looked to you as his mother more than his maternal one. Kenthap would have had to set about trying to have you killed to keep Djer close to her when he started to rule. That would have created a whole new mess when they found out what you are. Don't you see, it worked out for the best? All you have to do now is let it go, let it become a memory. Another one in your huge reservoir."

Lady Challis rested her forehead on her knees and she felt her eyes fill with water, but the tears did not flow as they had before. She raised her head and rubbed her eyes, forcing the liquid in them to run down on to her cheeks. She looked away from Amunet concentrating on Machu Picchu. Slowly she shook her head. One of the brightly attired nobles was lying face down on the ground, a club a few feet from his open, grasping hand. Standing over him, gesturing with his club, another noble.

"Looks like that one standing struck the one on the ground from behind and smashed his skull."

Amunet turned and looked where Lady Challis was staring.

"I have his soul now." She sighed,

"Humans. He had cancer; he would have died very soon. The one standing killed him to save him from the pain. The dead was his son."

The clacking of a man's shoes on the tiled floor in the corridor brought her back to reality. She wondered how, after the death of that Inca nobleman she had never met, she had left her thoughts until now. Was it a sign? She straightened her black diamond ring.

"Lady Challis!" Manual exclaimed.

"Lady Challis!" He repeated.

He bowed rather stiffly thought Lady Challis as he went down on one knee close to her chair. She held out her hand with her ring. He received her hand gently with both hands as if he were cupping water to drink. He touched the ring to his forehead, then over each eye and finally he kissed it at length. Like a precious gift, he set her hand back on the arm of her chair.

"Lady Challis, how may I be of service?" He asked looking down at the tiles on the balcony floor.

Lady Challis reached out and brushed loose strands of hair back on his head. She heard him inhale as she did so.

"You can start by looking up at me, look me in the eye when you speak to me. We have known each other long enough that you do not need to study grout in the tiles when you speak to me."

Manuel looked up.

"Thank You!"

"You have not taken another wife since Ximena?"

"My Lady, Ximena, left a hole in my heart that cannot be filled by just anyone. I count myself very fortunate to have found one so special."

Lady Challis sniffed the air casually; she sensed the pheromone Manual gave off.

"You are still human, there will be a time when you will become one of us and there is no one better than a wife from our kind to bite you." Lady Challis breathed deeply.

"It has been a long time since I gave advice on matters of the heart, but I am sure I can find someone for you." She reached out and patted Manuel on the arm.

"Now let's have breakfast. I am starving."

Barefoot, Lady Challis moved to the long table. Manual hurried to straighten her serving place and make the table layout as perfect as possible until Lady Challis stopped him. She moved past him and sat down opposite to where he would be sitting.

The maid reappeared with a breakfast cart laden with traditional Portuguese bread, butter, several types of ham, cheeses, jam, and black coffee. She moved to serve Manuel but he held up his hand to stop her.

"Doroteia, No!" He pointed to Lady Challis.

"This is Lady Challis; she must always be served first."

Lady Challis reached out for the carafe of coffee and started filling Manuel's cup and then her own as she looked up at Doroteia.

"Just do whatever you are accustomed to. I do not need to be served first, and you will need two fresh carafes of coffee." Then, she turned to the cart and started to fill her plate by herself.

"I appreciate what you say and your intentions, Manuel, but sometimes all I need is my plate filled with good food and my cup filled with wonderful coffee." She looked down and started to eat.

As the maid cleaned away the breakfast and left two more carafes of coffee, Lady Challis cradled her cup in her hands and looked around at the potted plants abundant with flowers of all kinds, but she thought, a woman's touch is required here. The colours were haphazard and unorganized. Different heights of plants and their different pots led to a rampage of oddities.

"Lady Challis, if I may. The latest financial returns and growth…" Manual stopped speaking as Lady Challis waved him to silence.

"Manuel, I know the numbers I saw the projections. That is not why I am here … we are to discuss your next role."

Manuel frowned and opened his mouth as if to speak, but then closed it without a sound. His hands nervously started to straighten the table cloth.

"There are some vampires in the company that have shown some, shall we say, dislike the role I am playing now."

Lady Challis put her cup down.

"Because you are human?"

"Yes. My Lady." Manual's mannerism changed; he was more assertive and clearer in his words. The table cloth was suddenly jerked straight.

Without realizing she was copying Manuel; she started to straighten the table cloth on her side of the table.

"Call a senior management and board of directors meeting for later this afternoon. I will open their eyes." Her fingers moved from straightening the table cloth to folding her napkin.
"This house is company property?"

"Yes."

"Do you like it?"

"Yes."

"It is yours. I will have the title transferred by end of day…"

"Err. Lady Challis, property transfers still take weeks. But thank you very much," Manuel sat up straight and leaned forward.

Lady Challis refilled her coffee cup,

"Connections, Manuel. Connections. It will be done when our meeting ends."

16.   The Ghost of the Steppes

Elect-Si stared down at the clear mirror like water. The sun was not up yet but there was enough light for her sharp eyes to see her reflection. As her legs moved slowly in the Reflecting Lake, the ends of her long kaftan drifted in the water as if watching her feet.

"It was odd," she said as if to no one in particular, but she knew Gwendoline was standing a few feet away, her feet hovering a few inches above the surface of the lake soaking up the coolness of water.

"I was there. You didn't see me; I was in the second line of your men." Replied Gwendoline a she shook her waist-length white hair behind her.

"No, I didn't see you." She looked up at the first pale orange streamers of the rising sun. But in the eyes of her mind, the sun was already up and its fierce heat was starting to be felt on all those on the dusty earth of the herdsman's track. The trail came up off the dark green grass of the endless Mongolian steppe and started to meander through the hills like a snake between several low hills.

A caravan of western traders and merchants looked nervously at the Mongol horsemen lined up, two, and three deep on the hills to their left and right. In front, a few Mongols with an older man who held a strange round tote on a pole.

Sven looked down the dusty track to where they had just come. Several small dust plumes hung in the air to one side of the caravan. Merchants who in panic had left the caravan, abandoned their goods and started running in blind fear. The sunlight drove harshly through the dust suspended above their arrow laden corpses.

A golden eagle let out a piercing screech, its wings slamming against the air as it landed on the outstretched arm of a Mongol rider on a hill to the right. Everyone's eyes were on the rider, who was now gently stroking the eagle's chest.

"They call her the Eagle General. She is a very powerful general in the army of The Great Lord Chinggis Khan." The voice standing next to him was shaded and muffled but authoritative and knowing.

"How do you know that?

"There is only one such general; her reputation is known widely. Remember, we are on their land. You need to know such things. I am surprised you do not,"

"Their land, this is the road to China and great riches; does it pass through their lands?"

"It does and their land you call it, as if it is nothing, we have been riding and walking on it for two months."

"So, what are they going to do with us? Kill us?"

"Probably."
"Why are they waiting, if that is what they are going to do, they should get it over with?"

"Do you like this day so little that you want to have your eyes closed right now? Who knows? We may not have to die. It is a possibility I would rather think about that than the one you rush towards."

"I am not rushing towards anything I just want whatever is to happen, to be quick."

"I have an idea, Mario. One of the traders has slave girls. Perhaps we can trade them for our lives. He says some are virgins. The one with the long dark hair, you know, the pretty one. He says she is a virgin but I don't think so. Since we joined the caravan, he has used her many times. And there are young boys too. Maybe they would like a soft-fleshed boy. I will go and suggest this idea; it is a good one."

"Wait … stop. There is a rider coming with many men. Look. Down the trail."

"Look where … oh! I see. Now we are really fucked!"

"Can this get any worse? Who is that? The one with the long fair hair."

"They call her the Ghost of the Steppe. She commands the Great Lord's personal guard, elite troops. On the battle field, they are like a bolt of lightning that brings death."

"Now they have stopped, I can see her face; she is not one of them; the skin is much paler, and the features are western, like Italian women I knew at home."

"You only knew whores. Make sure you do not mention that to her or speak of it."

"Heaven above, look at that gold necklace … it is the size of both my hands together."

"It is from the Great Lord; it tells the world who she is and that she speaks in his name. Make sure you bow when she walks by."

" … and if I do not?"

"Your knees will become your feet."

"She has one long sword and one short sword; they are just tucked into the sash at her waist."

"Fuck! You know nothing. That cloth is the black banner of the Great Lord's army; they march under it."

"I think she is coming over. Oh! Three of her troops are getting down as well. They are drawing swords."

"If you are going to comment on everything, look up at the hill. Some archers have come to do the hill. They have arrows nocked and are ready to fire. Which of your eyes are you blind in?"

From behind, a commotion erupted. A woman screaming, the sound of shackles and chains and the thud of something hitting the ground and the sound of it being dragged.

"Ha, Yousef must have figured out my plan all by himself. He has the pretty one. Ahh, she has fallen and he is dragging her by her neck. I think he is going to offer her to the Ghost for her men to use in exchange for his freedom. Now he is making her stand by pulling on her hair and screaming at her."

"Maybe there is a chance for us to be treated better."

"What are you doing, combing your hair, trying to make yourself look beautiful?"

"Just getting the dust out. Look she is coming this way."

"She is shouting at Yousef, who is dragging the girl again."

"Mother of all the saints and the Virgin Mary, did you see that!"

"I did, but my eyes cannot measure it."

"The long sword was unsheathed and swung and then back into the scabbard. The motion was so beautiful and elegant. Fluid like water running over rocks."

"Yousef is screaming, look, she took his hands with that one swing of her blade. He just has stumps now … why do they not bleed more than they do? Do you know?"

"The Ghost is calling over some of her men. Giving them instructions. Can you make out what she is saying?"

"No, I cannot hear, but look now. Two of them stripped Yousef. Such a body, I cannot look at it … you would need fingers and toes to count the sores on his back. That poor girl, being expected to hold on to him as he used her."

"They are walking him to the edge of the track where the boulders are? Laying him down, are they going to leave him there?"

"Yes, but look at that other one, he is bringing rocks about the size of Yousef's head. Cover your ears, I think I know what they are going to do."

"What are they going to do? Oh, by the blessed Virgin Mary, they are crushing his knees."

"No hands, unable to run or walk, naked, the wild animals will eat him alive as soon as we leave."

"Wait ... wait. The ghost is coming back this way. She is coming over to us. Oh shit, she has pulled out the small sword."

"She cut off your shirt and looked at the scratches tattooed on your skin. She looked at the hammer you wear on a leather cord around your neck."

"These scratches may have saved our lives. They are runes; it is the way my people write; this is Thor's Hammer; he is a great good to me and my people."

"Horses, a soldier is bringing us horses. We are to ride in style. Wherever you come from, I thank you."

"You are welcome."

"So. I was the Ghost of the Steppe? And I did all of that in clear sight of the mother, and you, I have never been to Mongolia; I have never lived in that time."

Gwendoline looked at Elect-Si as she slowly turned her face to the spreading sunlight to drink in its warmth. Then she slowly walked over to where Elect-Si was sitting and sat down, allowing her feet to break the surface of the lake and play in the water.

"You have to accept that so much about you is unexplainable. You did not live at that time; there is no Ghost of the Steppe in Mongol history. It was a way of allowing your spirit, the white and black in you, to have free rein in a place and time when doing what was done required no explanation other than you gave the order."

"So, it was a test?"

"Look at it this way. You acted and gave justice and punishment to another black shaman. What would your justice and your punishment be like when humans were involved and you thought of yourself as a human. The darkness you faced was not so dark. Nothing more than one human being despicable to another."

"So, it was a test?"

Gwendoline let out a long sigh and splashed the water with her feet.

"If it was a test? Did I pass?"

"There is no pass, no fail. You have an eternity of decisions to make; consistency will allow you to look at each and be satisfied."

"Do you regret any of your decisions? You are immortal, like Challis?"

Gwendoline did not look at Elect-Si.

"Yes, like you and Challis, I am immortal. But a long time ago…" she paused.

"So incredibly long ago… I decided I would not, could not be involved in the affairs of our kind … or humans the way you and Challis are."

"You were afraid of making decisions and giving out punishment."

Gwendoline stood up slowly, her feet once again a few inches above the water. She looked over at the orange disk of the sun peeping over the edge of the mountains; then she brushed some stray strands of her white hair back from her face.

"My…" she seemed to be groping for words.

"My judgments and punishment had no balance. There was never consistency."

"… And I am?"

"Consistent."

17. Petr

Petr gazed up at the starry night sky and began counting the constellations he could see. Those were the days when he was a kid, counting stars under a clear sky. As he grew up and headed to university, he got a telescope and set it up so he could lie on the ground and look through the eyepiece. It wasn't the best way to watch the night sky; sometimes he fell asleep, but it was better than anything else he could think of.

He rolled over and found himself perfectly aligned behind his sniper rifle. Muffled with a silencer, painted black and covered with black netting, twigs, and leaves, he knew he could not be seen. He was sighted on the back door of the old building his brother had died in and where he had been wounded, met Elect-Si, and the other vampires of her kind.

As he thought of the vampire blood coursing through his veins, the invigorating, powerful energy in it gave him a sense of being able to do what he wanted, when he wanted. He had not felt that way since his youth. The fact there were two genres of vampire and a subtle war was being carried out between them stimulated him and gave him a purpose he had not felt since joining the military police.

He was on one side of the battle and was determined to bring the other side to its knees and obedient to Lady Challis and Elect-Si.

His earpiece crackled with a code word that told him his comrades were in position.

He flipped his wrist over and looked at the luminous hands of his watch. Two minutes. One minute and then the door slowly opened.

One of Dorion's meat cutters slipped through the half-open door, her plastic apron glittering in the moonlight from the blood on it, with the new intensity of his vampire eyesight and the clarity of the sniper scope, he could see the liquid dripping on to the ground. She was followed by two more. The last nun wedged a few bricks conveniently left by the door to keep it open. She had a lit cigarette in her fingers. The others were fishing under their aprons for cigarettes and a lighter. He focused on the nun closest to the door, and pulled the trigger.

It took a few seconds for the bullet to cover the distance from his rifle to the back of the head of that bitch, but the result was what he hoped it would be. The back of her head exploded. She slumped to the ground, immediately her remaining brain poured out. The other two at first did not notice; they were too busy opening a new packet of cigarettes.

Finally! The cigarettes were unwrapped and the top flipped open. The holder of the cigarette packet suddenly squeezed it, sending cigarettes in a strange arc of white pinpoints of light as she fell backward on to a pile of broken, disused bricks.

The last of them used the flame of her lighter stare at her fallen companion. But almost as her knee touched the ground, she realized she was bleeding from a gunshot she had never heard. She half turned to look around to raise the alarm when a second bullet tore off the front of her face as it ripped through her cheek and out the other side.

She remained kneeling holding up the lighter; the flame went out as it arced overhead. He refocused and sent another bullet into her through where he thought her ear was. The head dress flipped up at the back, as if some invisible mischievous boy had run by and flipped it up to annoy the nun. In the cold white light of the moonlight, he could see hair and large splashes of blood explode out from under it on to the ground and the nun rolled away to land on her shoulder.

From the undergrowth armed men, his brothers in arms erupted and moved quickly and silently to the open door. The first slipped inside to secure it and was followed by several more very quickly. The last stopped to push the door further open and jammed it by wedging more bricks under it and then moved to a position where he could fire on anyone coming through the door.

Petr started to move but a hand pushed him firmly back on to the ground.

"Don't move! Look for the unexpected, the unplanned. You are here to cover them." Hissed Miray.

"Top wall left corner. Cigarette."

Petr rolled back behind his rifle and focused on the wall where Miray indicated. Yes, another nun taking a cigarette break! He focused on her face, so young, such a beautiful face. He saw her draw heavily on the cigarette, causing the tip to glow brightly and illuminate the lower part of her face. Slowly she took the cigarette from her lips and let it start to drift out of her mouth. Suggestively, as if about to suck a man, she wrapped her lips around the smoke that hung at her lips … she was breathing it in as a bullet entered her mouth with the cloud of smoke and ripped out the back of her head.

"Now, we can join those inside." Said Miray as she held the microphone of a small transmitter to her mouth.

"Ten nuns accounted for," reported his Sargent as they entered.

"The cages? How many?"

"The cages are empty, but there are two containers at the loading dock, each half full of frozen bodies from the war."

Miray and Petr moved into the cutting room. Several nuns lay sprawled on the floor, their bodies exploded by precisely placed rounds. Headless bodies hung up by their ankles or wrists, dripping their blood into troughs.

"Why are the troughs so wide now?" Muttered Petr.

"Looking at the ceiling, it has been reinforced. I am guessing they are hanging two bodies off each meat hook." Replied Miray.

"The heads are being processed separately; cranial fluid is being sold as a morning tonic, tongue-in-cheek meat for BBQs."

They moved on.

"… and this?" Asked one of Petr's men moving around pre-packaged leg meat with what looked like a toupee in an attached sealed pouch.

"It's a new trend, a hobby, collecting the scalps of the humans they are eating."

Petr stood still for a moment, his hand to his earpiece.

"There is something interesting in the loading dock. We should go and see."

18.   Superior General Phaedra

Phaedra sat on a heavy old wooden office chair that had been dragged from the loading dock manager's office. She flipped the illuminated page of her bible over slowly as she studied the beautiful workmanship. The bandaged finger of her right hand throbbed with the movement and then calmed down as she rested it.

When the page was turned, her fingers went back to the heavy gold crucifix resting on her breasts sitting like fluffy clouds above her black leather bustier.

A high-heeled shoe dangled precariously off her big toe completely unaware of its possible fate on the floor. Her voluminous leather pants were are relaxed as she was.

Around her head a broad gold chain, like a halo, held a gold crucifix in the middle of her forehead. Studied with a red ruby at its centre, it glittered in the factory lighting.

To her right, half in the shadows a stocky heavy old man stood partly resting on his cane and partly on the wall behind him.

A foot or so from the Superior General, Cassius rolled slowly. Naked, he had been emasculated, dried blood was congealed and hardened on the undressed stitches that sealed his wound. Bound tightly with barbed wire and gagged, he tried desperately to find a position in which his body did not know pain.
Miray moved into the space cautiously. Petr's men had the scene surrounded one directly behind Phaedra, one targeting the old man and two other snipers on the high cat walks. Two men guarded the back doors of the refrigeration containers pressed up against their loading docks.

Phaedra looked up at the group entering; she slowly shut her bible and closed the lock on the good book and smiled thinly.

"I had expected to be greeted by Vicereine Elect-Si. But you will do."

"Why did you hope to see Elect-Si?"

"Negotiate."

"Elect-Si will negotiate with Sophyra, not you. You are Superior General of an Order that orders from Dorion."

Phaedra stared coldly at Miray.

"Spoken like a soldier."

"Soldier? Yes, I am, and proud of it."

"No disrespect intended. Soldiers recognize the chain of command and follow orders, that is all I meant." Phaedra paused and looked over to the old man in the shadows.

"My father."

The old man shuffled out into the light.

"What do you want?"

"I do not want… I expect. I expect you to carry a message to Vicereine Elect-Si. It needs to be clear and unambiguous." Phaedra slipped her foot into her shoe and flicked her foot in the direction of Casius, the heel of her shoe skidded off his forehead and then dug in on the side of his face and pushed his head to one side, making him moan as the barbed wire dug into his shoulders.

"Dear Cassius. His army fuels and sustains the war, producing more human corpses for harvesting than can be consumed by Sophyra's kind. I suspect you, or Challis, or Elect-Si had something to do with creating the army."

"It stopped Sophyra harvesting locally. If there are too many corpses, that is your problem, your war."

"At some future time, decided by Vicereine Elect-Si, the army would turn on Sophyra and eliminate as many of her kind as you could identify. The war would end." Phaedra leaned forward slightly and looked down at Casius,

"Isn't that right? My fucking toy?"

Cassius grunted into his gag.

"I will take that as a yes." Phaedra looked at Miray.

"Casius gave me an inventory of Sophyra's kind in the high echelons of both papacies. Not as many as expected?" Phaedra waited for a reply but Miray said nothing.

"What is the message you want me to deliver to Elect-Si?"

"Don't be so impatient; there are certain rituals to this meeting that must be adhered to. They provide a certain flow to this gathering."

"Really?"

"Yes." Phaedra sighed and slowly stood up, as she did, she kicked the heavy chair backward. The casters on the chair screeched at the demand to move quickly and then the chair abruptly stopped. It teetered on two wheels and then fell over, pulling hard on two thin cords attached to the legs. Casius convulsed violently on the floor and made ferocious gurgling sounds into his gag as he thrashed around without regard for the barbed wire. A large pool of blood spreads from his neck across the floor as Phaedra's garotte sliced through his neck. A few seconds later his body stopped thrashing and his head rolled to one side without its firm connection to his torso.

"There, all done! Now, we can get down to business."

Cautiously, looking at Miray, Petr, and the guards closest to her, Phaedra reached into her pocket. She took out a small glass bottle and removed the secure lid. Looking up, she noted an overhead light and moved into it. She held the first and second fingers over the neck of the bottle. As Miray watched, a clear liquid formed at the tip of her nails and sparkled in the overhead light as it dripped into the bottle.

"There," said Phaedra as she screwed the top on and set the bottle on the floor.

"A couple of teaspoons of shall we say snake venom. Enough for your scientists to determine what I am." She straightened and reached back into her pocket and pulled out a clear plastic bag, sealed at the top. Inside was a finger nail.

"You will need this to understand the full scope of what the liquid means." She wiggled her bandaged finger at Miray.

"It's mine if there are any questions."

"Why are you doing this?"

"Why? Allowing Sophyra to ascend to the Papacy in the east and another of her kind in the west were mistakes." Phaedra's eyes flared at Miray. She waved her hand…

"Oh, I can see why it happened. I can see why you and Vicereine Elect-Si chose to do what you did." Phaedra held a finger to her chin as if in feigned thought. After a few moments, she looked up at Miray,

"Well … maybe not." She turned to look at Casius's body.

"What is that military saying: no battle plan survives contact with the enemy? But that is for a discussion when I meet the Vicereine." Phaedra half turned to look at her father.

"Test the liquid in that bottle, study the nails and set up a meeting. For now, my father and I will be leaving through that door." She started to walk towards her father, who was already shuffling towards the messenger's exit, but she paused and looked back at Casius; she blew his body a breathy kiss.

19.   A New Vampire Appears

Elect-Si slipped her tablet showing analysis and presentations on Phaedra to one side and went back to stroking the long fur of her new kitten, which rested peacefully on her lap.

As she watched the kitten jump off her legs, she yawned and rubbed her eyes.

"Wellington! So, you knew of this genre of vampire?" She looked across the verandah at the elf, who stood reading his own tablet.

"I knew stories about them; they were part of our oral tradition. Parents would tell their children about them to scare them and keep them home at night. I never saw one, I never met anyone who had." He tapped the screen of his tablet.

"Venom. One of our stories tells how one of these vampires was bitten by a venomous snake. The poison injected by the snake's fangs was changed by the vampire as it entered the blood stream and did not kill them. It became part of the liquid vampires used by humans."

He turned the tablet off and stood militarily correct as he looked out across the abundant flowers at the verandah's railing towards the reflecting lake.

"It was said they sharpened their finger nails so they could scratch the person they wanted to inject with liquid. The enzymes pass through channels within the nails into the scratch. They could either turn a human into a being they could feed off regularly, a vampire, or simply kill them." He turned and looked at Lady Challis, who was bent over looking at a vibrant new flower, and Elect-Si now seated upright on her easy chair.

"They did not, do not, eat humans."

Lady Challis stood up and, without turning, spoke to Wellington.

"To kill a human, was it the snake venom activated somehow."

Wellington's lips moved as if he were saying something to himself, then he looked at Lady Challis.

"I was just singing a childhood rhyme to myself. My mother used to sing it and make me repeat it back to her so she knew I had remembered it." He cleared his throat.

"This is the relevant part, I think. A young boy threw a stone, not a big one, not a small one, one just right in size to leave a black mark and hurt the vampire fishing at the boy's favourite fishing hole … the vampire chased and chased the boy until he caught him. He scratched the arm of the boy and golden liquid from the vampire's nail mixed with the boy's blood… The boy died as if bitten by a snake."

"Wellington, what colour was the snake in the rhyme?"

"It was a Yellow Cobra."

"Sounds like the Cape Cobra. A variation of the cobra species." Said, Lady Challis.

"I knew them well when I was living in Afrika."

"So, now there are three types of vampires; we bite, Sophyra spits, and Phaedra scratches." Summarized Elect-Si.

Lady Challis started to pace slowly along the edge of the verandah, stopping to look at flowers.

"We didn't know of Sophyra; why should we know of Phaedra?"

Wellington cleared his throat.

"May I ask whether this Phaedra is still castrating young men and sending them off to war? And why did she castrate and kill Cassius?"

Miray stepped on to the verandah from a servant's door.

"Cassius tested positive for her venom, large quantities of it. He must have been one of their kind for a while." Miray paused.

"There was another set of enzymes in his blood. Sophyra's."

"Have you checked his finger nails?" asked Lady Challis. "Yes, a similar honey comb pattern to Phaedra's sample. Two finger nails on each hand had venom sacks, though the venom in them was very dilute compared to hers."

"We know Sophyra doesn't have wings. Does Phaedra?" asked Wellington.

Elect-Si turned her head to look at the elf.

"Are you thinking she is a completely different species of vampire?"

Wellington turned to look at Elect-Si.

"I lived in the time of Darwin. Toward the end of his life, to be precise. I met him at the British Museum. Splendid gentleman. He gave me a copy of his book. He did me the honour of signing it before handing it over. It seems to me that her you and her ladyship represent one branch of evolution, Sophyra another, and now we have a third. We know Sophyra has no fangs and no wings. Phaedra injects venom through her nails and can modify the enzymes rather like you. If she has wings, it seems she is closer to her ladyship and your good self than Sophyra."

"Are you proposing we try and form an alliance against Sophyra based on species?"

"No. I am saying we need to understand how you, not me, for I am not a vampire, have evolved and whether there is a fourth kind of vampire we do not know of. There was little awareness of Sophyra's kind and none of Phaedra's."

Elect-Si turned to her mother.

"We don't know what Phaedra's agenda is."

"Shall I make arrangements to have her here?" Asked Miray.

Lady Challis stared at Wellington,

"You met Darwin and have a signed copy of his book! "On the Origin of Species. Really."

Wellington seemed to grow in stature as re replied.

'Yes, and a copy of "The Descent of Man."

"The descent of Man. Both signed," repeated Lady Challis.

"Yes."

"I have been searching for an original signed copy of each for centuries." Lady Challis started walking towards Wellington with a broad smile on her face, which seemed to make the elf blush.

"Mother! Focus, Miray needs an answer."

Lady Challis stopped and looked at Elect-Si, the smile fixed on her face.

"Miray! Bring Phaedra here if she can be spared from her duties." Then she moved towards Wellington.

20.   Xemina

"Manuel. I have a question to ask you. Be honest, and be frank. Hold nothing back." Lady Challis slipped her arm into Manuel's and held his hand softly. But in doing so, she started to guide their steps to the abundant flowers by the reflecting lake.

"This palace is so majestic; the plants are fantastic. I could spend a lifetime amongst them. You know since our walk in your gardens, and seeing the Black Roses, I have spent most of my free hours studying all types of flowers." Manual smiled at Lady Challis.

"Thank you for doing that at such a bad time in my life."

"It was my pleasure and I am pleased you have found a new hobby. But I still need to find a woman to keep you in bed, screaming at the top of your lungs as you make passionate love, the way you did with Ximena."

Manual stumbled at the frankness of her ladyship's words. She held on to his hand and arm to steady him.

"My Lady, I did not know our intimate secrets were known by yourself."

"They are not, I am just guessing." They walked on in silence for several minutes, stopping here and there to look at blooms and to admire the view.

"Manuel, did you bring that picture of Ximena?"

"Yes." Manuel pulled out his phone and indicated the home screen that had a picture of Ximena. Her left hand with long sharp, black painted nails cradled it as she tried to turn his face towards hers so she could kiss him on camera.

"Manuel. Did she ever scratch you; those nails look ferociously sharp."

Manuel looked at the image for a few moments before returning the device to his pocket. He paused and looked out across the lake,

"Yes, often. We used to laugh about it." Manuel sighed.

"Sex was vigorous and often. They make jokes about being able to see stars when you have a passionate partner. But I was lucky; with Ximena, I saw a galaxy of stars."

"I guess you are talking about sleeping on the large balcony of your house." Lady Challis grinned at Manual.

"We had a thick, king-size futon. We had pillows, sheets, and old-style wool blankets. After we had sex, we would lay there covered, all snuggled, and look up at the stars." Manuel paused for several minutes.

"Then we did it all again… It was exhausting but so very enjoyable."

"I can see why you have been single for so long after her death. It would be hard to find another wife, like Ximena, so passionate, beautiful, and intelligent." Lady Challis guided their steps down towards the lake.

"Tell me, after she scratched you, did you ever feel like scratching someone else, perhaps one of those people at the company that mistreated you?"

Manuel stopped walking and half turned to Lady Challis.

"I felt like killing them. Scratching occurred to me once but I could not fathom how that would kill them; it seemed such a mild thing to do. Besides, there was a problem with that idea. I simply could not bring myself to do it."

"Why is that?"

Manuel held out his free hand for Lady Challis to look at.

"I have a condition, Anonychia Congenita; I was born without finger or toe nails. I cannot scratch anyone if I wanted to."

Lady Challis froze in her step. Stunned at what she was seeing. Quickly she flipped over Manuel's other hand, the one she was holding, and studied the finger tips where nails should have been.

"I…. I … had never noticed."

"Most people do not. There is nothing wrong with my fingers; they are as dexterous as any other person, and they are as sensitive when touching things."

Lady Challis looked up from Manuel's hand but held it more firmly.

"Shall we continue back to the palace; we need to get ready for dinner."

"Of course, my Lady."

"Call me Anastasia."

21.   Blood and Love

Miray turned her tablet over to Lady Challis.

"I am sorry, I should have read the full report on Manuel's blood. I only read the cover page."

Lady Challis flipped through the rest of the report.

"Traces of venom, a little of his wife's vampire enzymes, not enough to make him one, nothing more." Lady Challis put down the tablet and rubbed her temples.

"When I held the meeting in Lisbon, several vampires said they could sense Ximena was a vampire, but somehow, she was different. They didn't find out how different. Eventually it led to a fight, literally, a fight. She won easily. Later, they killed her and made it look as if humans had done it."

"What I find interesting is that Ximena married a human and did not convert him to one of her kind. Even with his condition, she could have sired him and had an extended and loving life with him. We would never do that; we would make a human one of our kind, and then marry them." Miray took a deep breath.

"I have no idea what Sophyra's kind would do."

"Eat them," smiled Lady Challis with a little chuckle, "Like a praying mantis."

A servant appeared with white gloves holding a silver platter on which was a folded piece of cream vellum paper, blue ink hand-writing clearly visible on it. He offered the note to Lady Challis.

Lady Challis opened it and read quickly.

"Miray, where the fuck is Petr?"

"I left him at the processing plant to supervise the clean-up. Why?"

Lady Challis handed the message to Miray.

"Dorion and a small force arrived after you and Phaedra left. Petr and his men were all killed, but he managed to kill Dorion. One of her nuns killed Petr moments later."

Lady Challis dropped the note and clapped her hands loudly.

"Notice the initial at the bottom, "P," I assume that is Phaedra.' Lady Challis breathed a sigh of relief.

"I am glad Dorion is gone."

"That places Phaedra one step from the Papacy in the East…" Said Wellington emerging on to the balcony, a large leather-bound book under his arm.

Lady Challis turned and looked at the elf.
"The tips of your ears may have been docked, but your hearing is as good as any elf I have ever met."

Wellington shrugged and tapped the book.

"The log book of HMS Beagle for the period Darwin was in the Galapagos. But, if you want to know my thoughts, I think the sequence of events at the processing plant was fortuitous, but hardly an accident."

"Phaedra planned it?" asked Miray.

"Sophyra and her kind have repeatedly shown naked aggression in achieving their goals. Phaedra and hers, well, let's say they seem to be equally aggressive but they like to work in the shadows. They seem more…" he looked at Lady Challis,

"Like you, my lady."

Lady Challis moved closer to Wellington and reached out to touch the book.

"The log book … how many more books do you have from Darwin and the voyage?"

"A few."

"Go on, you have something to add about Phaedra."

Wellington moved the book so it was further under his arm and away from Lady Challis's roving hand.

"Opportunists. She is an opportunist. I believe they do not necessarily want the Papacy." He looked at Lady Challis to see if his last words raised a response from her.

"Go on…."

"They want control, not ownership. They are patient, as patient as you m'lady."

"Control, not ownership." Repeated Lady Challis.

Wellington gave a polite cough, but seemed to stand more erect, with his head back and chest out, more of a military parade ground posture.

"Lady Challis, you wanted a woman to be Pope, just as you witnessed your friend a millennium ago. You anticipated … hoped, it would be you. Sophyra wanted it for herself so she could control the fate of humans and the lust her kind has for human flesh." Wellington paused and adjusted his shoulders.

"Bodies from the war fed the demand for flesh. It stopped the harvesting of small rural, peasant populations in Europe."

"And Dorion? She controlled Phaedra and Cassius." Interrupted Miray.

Wellington took the book out from under his arm and held it in front of him.

"Evolution. Change, through procreation and adaptation. You forget the power of the female womb. Neither you nor Elect-Si were in Cassius's bed. He wanted to have children and Phaedra was a convenient womb. He wanted to breed, as the priests say. He had no idea what she was; she controlled him completely."

"Dorion?" Questioned Lady Challis.

"Setting Dorion and Petr against each other in a pitched battle was the best way to eliminate her. Petr was a tool, a means to an end. His death is an accident. But, beyond the moment, I do not see a need for him."

Wellington read the quizzical expression on Lady Challis's face.

"Don't you see? With him dead, there is no one in the local militia who knows about vampires, the Eastern Pope and all our plans. No one knows the true reason for the war." Wellington looked out over the lake.

"The processing plant was some ghastly abomination created by a depraved quasi-religious order. No one in the militia hierarchy will believe any of it. They will destroy it and forget about it."

"So, Phaedra set up Petr's the conditions for the raid and lured Dorion to the processing plant knowing a battle would happen." Lady Challis turned to look at Miray.

"Petr came to me proposing the raid and asked me to participate. He wanted me to bring additional men, transports, and weapons. I agreed. Destroying the facility would make Sophyra more dependent on the facility in Anatolia; we have better insight there." Said Miray slowly.

Wellington moved the book under his other arm to the side away from Lady Challis.

"Phaedra was there with her father and Cassius. Cassius had been tortured, emasculated, and bound with barbed wire. The heavy old chair had been set up so tipping it over would engage her garotte and cut Cassius's throat. She was prepared, Miray."

Lady Challis moved to admire an orchid and then turned to look at Wellington,

"Phaedra cannot control Sophyra. She cannot control me; she cannot control Elect-Si. So, who then?"

Wellington's eyes moved to the distant Himalayas; his mind deep in thought. Finally, he turned his attention back to Lady Challis.

"Manuel, he needs a wife. He has had one of her Phaedra's kind before." Slowly he took the book from under his arm.

"Shall we read this together?" he said, offering the book to Lady Challis.

Lady Challis frowned at Wellington.

"Manuel is human; there has never been a married pope while in office. Adrian II in the Nineth Century would be the closest. There have been many sexually active popes. How would we control the Pope if he goes to bed with Phaedra every night?"

"That is for Elect-Si and Phaedra to work out." He turned to look at Lady Challis.

"When you asked the question, how would we control Phaedra, you really meant you. You are still too invested in ownership." Slowly he took the book from under his arm and held it in front of him.

"Do you still want to read this with me?"

"Yes, very much."

A watery yellow sun crept nervously into the sky, like a party goer still drunk from the night's revelling, it lingered in its own brightness at the edge of the reflecting lake. A gentle breeze covered the water kicking up some ripples that caressed the nipples and thighs of a woman lying naked on the surface of the warm water.

Slowly the person floating turned over and started to swim to the steps.

As the woman walked up the steps from the lake, a cane moved around her as if inspecting her. The cane hovered while the woman picked up a towel and towelled herself dry. She put on a thick white robe and pulled the belt tight around her waist. She followed the cane to the top of the steps and to its owner's hand. A hand extended and grasped the cane. Long, flowing black lace attached to an equally long and flowing black dress. An intricately carved cameo broch at the throat, and then the very long white hair.

"You must be Gwendoline."

"You are Phaedra."

"Do you always welcome guests while they have nothing on?"

"You were such an inviting and very different opportunity. I could not resist." Gwendoline stood up.

"A suite has been prepared for you." She watched as Phaedra looked around the lake and the palace's reflection.

"I saw you land; your wings are very aerodynamic; they are built for speed."

"Thank you, beautiful, aren't they, like falcon's wings." She looked up to the top of the steps and at Amunet.

"Amunet helped enormously. It would have been hard to get here in one night if not her help controlling the wind."

"Falcon. So, you see yourself as a predator?"

Phaedra turned to look at Gwendoline and locked eyes with her,

"I am very much a predator. But you knew that already, didn't you?" There was a pause, silence only broken by the lapping of waves at the marble steps.

"They call you the Queen of All the North. You have held that title for so many millennia that no one challenges you now. A queen does not reign without being a hunter of all below her. So, we are alike in that regard."

Gwendoline moved a few steps higher, and turned to look down on Phaedra.

"That is true…" she said thoughtfully, and then continued up the steps.

Elect-Si pushed back the hood on her robe. She felt like Nostro Damas hunched over a bowl of mysterious fluid reading the future. She nudged the table as she moved her seat and water in the black-bottomed bowl rippled and moved from side to side angrily. She pinched the space between her eyes; the strain of concentrating for the past few minutes had been intense.

"You are trying too hard. Clear your mind. Relax and let your conscience wander."

She opened her eyes and turned to look in the direction of the voice. Her guide stood engrossed in the beautiful flowers and growing things at the verandah wall. He spoke without looking at her.

"Your ego is taking over. The challenges of these events trigger your intellect and you have lost your ability to be in the moment. Look and pay attention to how the events flow on a river of existence. Allow your essence to engage with the river." He turned to look at her.

"What do you think you will learn from the staring at crystal balls and into bowls of water?" He asked.

"I was hoping for guidance. Perhaps I was hoping to see the future." She paused and looked around the table at all the things she had gathered to try and help her divine how things could work out.

"If you were able to see the future, would it be a future you would like?"

"I am not sure. Can you show me the future?"

"No. I have no better ability to see the future than you. But I do not have an ego. I follow the moment and my conscience to engage with each other. Phaedra, your consciousness tell you about her."

"Not much. Only that she sees herself as a predator, and yet there is not much evidence of it."

"She is a predator, and if you are not careful, you will be her prey. A predator does not have to look like someone or something that is all claws and fangs. In fact, it is better they do no. That allows them to strike when it is unexpected and they do not have to expend energy to hunt prey without struggling."

"Do you think she will be an ally?" Asked Elect-Si tiredly.

"No, she will never be that."

"Should I write these predictions down?"

Her guide shrugged.

"There is not much point in doing so; events will move quickly now you are together and in the presence of your mother. One thing I will say is her kind are more numerous than you believe."

Elect-Si looked at the bowl of water she had been using to try and divine the future. It seemed to call to her; it beckoned her to break the clear mirror surface and to see what was under it.

She dipped her fingers in the water.

She twirled the water in slow lazy circles. For a moment, it seemed there was electricity in the water, and it searched for a way out. It found her fingers and passed down them into the muscles of her forearm and caused her muscles to twitch. In that moment, her mind opened and an avalanche of memories crashed out into her mind's eye. One held itself in the centre of her vision as the others cavorted around.

The memory was from the first few hours of her learning to fly. She had missed her footing as she came in to land; she tripped and crashed over on to one side. A sharp blow to her elbow sent shooting electric pulses up and down her arm. She had sat on a tall flat boulder, rubbing her elbow and flexing it to make sure she had not broken anything.

Her mind focused on the moment in the memory; she was suddenly aware she was conscious in the here and now and observing herself in that moment of the accident.

She could look down at herself and see a fallen angel and she could see herself looking back at herself hovering above. She was both the observer and the observed. Her consciousness moved back and forth effortlessly between the two perspectives. Slowly she became aware of a message being passed to her. Her mouth started to move without her considering what she was saying.

Abruptly Elect-Si took her fingers out of the water. and the electricity in her arm stopped; the memory faded with all the others. She stared at the water dripping off her finger tips and, one by one, licked the water off them.

"Phaedra is the balance point between our three species."

"It is good to see your consciousness expanding without help or judgment. Let it continue, do not limit it, let it go where it wants to go."

"In the last moment, I had a vision of a child's toy, a teeter-totter, one child goes up as one goes down. Sophyra was highest, always highest. She was looking around and then down at me and laughing. I could not get off the ground; my legs seemed not to have enough spring in them. If only I could have pushed up and she would have come down to my level … or beneath me." She paused as she studied the image in her mind of Sophyra, laughing.

"Then, I was on a teeter-totter with three seats. Phaedra was on a third seat. She could use her legs to help either Sophyra or myself. Phaedra was pushing to make Sophyra come down; it was working. But Phaedra was not using her legs to help me get any higher than being in balance." She looked at her guide.

"An interesting prediction. Especially for one who is the embodiment of balance between good and evil."

"Beware the three seats on the teeter-totter. You will always need someone in the third seat."
Elect-Si studied him as he turned back to look at the flowers.

22.   Phaedra

Lady Challis slowly closed the hard-worn leather bound book of Darwin's notes, and looked over at Phaedra.

"The turtle's shell … and the second voyage of the beagle… Darwin's finches. Evolution is the answer, isn't it? You knew all along."

Phaedra brushed away small ash flakes from her cigar that had fallen on her gold and black silk blouse. The movement made her braless breasts jiggle slightly under the fabric. She studied the cigar, rolling it between her fingers and then put it to her lips and took a long pull, making the end glow bright red. She looked sideways at Elect-Si and then back at Lady Challis. She exhaled the rich smoke and locked eyes with Lady Challis.

"For centuries … before Darwin…. But after Europeans landed in South America." She leaned forward to flip ash off her cigar into the silver ash tray. She moved the ash tray to the wide arm of the chair she was sitting in.

"Once we knew where Afrika was, some of my ancestors flew to look at it."

"You went to see if you could take the role of vampires in that ecosystem," said Elect-Si.

A thin smile crossed Phaedra's lips.

"Yes … we tried; it was difficult." She continued to look at Lady Challis.
"Except on the eastern coast, north Afrika, and of course, Egypt. Those were your domain … weren't they?"

"I never knew," murmured Lady Challis.

"We intended you didn't."

"Sophyra? Where did her species originate?" Asked Elect-Si.

"Southeast Asia," replied Phaedra without looking at her.

"After Afrika, we converted some European explorers to our kind and vigorously explored the globe on their backs." Phaedra flipped more ash into the ash tray.

"That is where we encountered them. They were aggressive and impulsive. They still are, as you know."

"Are you immortal?" Asked Lady Challis.

"Yes."

"So, you went to Afrika." It was a statement and a question at the same time.

"What did you see there that made you leave parts of it alone?"

"We didn't leave because of you; if that is what you are asking, we left large regions to you and your kind because we didn't want you to know about us." Phaedra picked up the ash tray and gently rolled the cigar tip around in it to clean the glowing tip.

"I saw you fake your death … after Narmer died, I saw you drown." Said Phaedra as she looked up.

"Cast your mind back, maybe when you are alone. There was a female passenger on a ferry that held your robe for a moment. It turned you over, from being face down and you looked at me. The sun had been up for a few hours. The breeze along the Nile was good for sailing and moving grain across from the Nile from the Eastern granary to the other side." Phaedra paused.

"A wind created by Amunet rocked the boat and a mule laden with grain sacks conveniently broke free and pushed you over the side. You passed under the ferry."

"Why did you do let go?"

"In the moment you looked at me, I realized what you were doing; I have always found faking my death so that I can move on to a new life, a new existence, to be the most difficult part of being immortal." Phaedra waved for her tumbler for a refill of Indian Rum.

"I shared your desire for it to be successful, especially in a time when you were grieving so deeply for Narmer."

Lady Challis inhaled deeply as old memories came flooding back. From the moment she allowed the mule with its unbalanced load to knock her over the side of the boat into the Nile, to climbing out downstream and into her new existence was all she had ever concentrated on. Now, the small details surfaced, passing under the ferry and her robe being tugged at on the other side came back to her.

Rolling over to briefly open her eyes to see what or who had snagged her. Was the snag an accident or a threat to her plan to appear to have drowned.

She rested her chin on her hand and stared at Phaedra. Comparing her face to the one in her memory was an exact match. The aquiline nose, the suggestive mouth, and the slightly pointed chin. The grey eyes, so very pale. The flicker of a smile that crossed the woman's lips as their eyes met and understanding passed between them. The tension in her robe and the hand gripping it. It seemed such a delicate hand and yet, so strong and powerful, holding her body weight against the fast flowing of the Nile in flood.

The rush of grasping male hands at the gunnels trying to clutch at the robe and pull her back to safety. Grasping in the hope of saving the noble woman, and getting a reward.

The woman holding the valuable robe being knocked to one side and letting go of the material that held Lady Challis and endangering her faked death.

"That was you. Yes! It was you!"

Phaedra shrugged.

"As soon as I realized what was happening, I allowed myself to be knocked over and let go of your robe." She raised her tumbler in a toast to Lady Challis.

Lady Challis sat fixed in the space of her memories. It raced through them and stopped. Her hand partly covering her mouth.

"A countess came to buy wine from my vineyard in Southern France. Just after my friend, the first Female Pope passed away. We spend hours talking of all minor things, like humans making small talk. Then you, it was you, wasn't it? Bought half of my favourite vintage."

"Good. You are starting to see the contacts we have had over the millennia."

"Why?"

"I like a good bottle of wine."

"No. Why"

"You needed to lighten up after she died. You had been grieving too deeply and too long for Narmer. It was … important to get to know you. Your goal of a female pope, you, was intriguing. Maybe it would help control the brutal persecution of indigenous people in South America by the Spanish and Portuguese." Phaedra adjusted her seating position. Her long black leather dress moved like a silky black wave. Bright sparks from crucifixes of blue diamonds, sapphires, and emerald crosses adorning the front panel sparkled vividly. "There was a certain synergy between your goal and an outcome we desired."

"You left and never came back."

"I like the goal and the plan and the ability to achieve it over time, but you were not open to changing it. You were not open to having a partner in that strategy."

"You are right on both counts." Lady Challis idly ran her fingers over the spine of the book she held. It seemed to have a message for her. She looked up at Phaedra, taking in the whole woman sitting there, smoking her cigar and drinking her liquor. This was not the fun conversation in her villa overlooking the Mediterranean.

"And yet you wear clothing decorated with crucifixes and carry a bible."

Phaedra's hand dropped to the book at her side, unconsciously, she stroked the spine.

"You are wondering about this. You want to read it."

"I have read the bible many times, and all the other religious books of the world."

"Yes, you have, haven't you! In the early 20th century, you studied religion at Cambridge. You ended up teaching religion there for an entire lifetime. So ironic, a vampire teaching religion to fresh-faced, wealthy, young aristocrats. How many graduated as vampires? Half, three quarters?

"There were many who became world leaders who took my courses." Lady Challis looked intently at Phaedra's eyes. The grey was so pale. How much she wondered did she know about her life?

"All of them. All who studied with me became vampires."

Phaedra started to chuckle at the answer, then she openly laughed out loud.

"Ever the ambitious bitch!"

Lady Challis glared at Phaedra.

"Several of them were very useful later."

Phaedra's lips lost their humour.

"It was not a criticism. I have done the same many times. But I did it in the jungle schools of the Amazon and the Andes."

Lady Challis looked to change the subject and her gaze landed back on the thick bible beside Phaedra and the large iridescent front panel of her dress.

"You are a vampire and yet you carry a bible and wear clothing with crosses on it."

Phaedra looked down at the jewelled front panel of her skirt, then to her bible. Her hand rested on its spine of the book and she patted it lightly.
"You want to read my bible." The words were spoken slowly and with great deliberation."

"Why not." Putting down her cigar, she lifted the book up and pressed her thumb and forefinger to the fingerprint scanner. The locks opened. She handed the book to a servant to give to Lady Challis.

Lady Challis studied the book. The cover was old, very old, the leather was thick and had been red stained when new, but now in many places, it was raw leather and it had been patched in several places. But it was also new technology; it was locked by a modern finger print reader. At the back, she could just see the edge of a pocket, for a tablet. The clasps were machined from titanium. Slowly she looked at the pages.

Page after page of ancient Latin, hand-written, probably in a monastery by a priest or nun copying from another work greeted her eyes. Beautiful glowing illuminations in full colour, still vibrant and very much alive, started some pages and completely filled others. Her fingers detected the pages were made of parchment, an ancient tradition of using the untanned skin of animals.

She moved forward in the book; there was a secret here that Lady Challis wanted to uncover but the book made searching difficult. The words changed to Greek, not just any Greek and ancient Greek. She inhaled sharply; this was the Greek from a time when she was at Sevastopol… and before that.

It had been three millennia since she had seen the beautiful language. Slowly, her lips moved as she cautiously mouthed some words. The material on which the Greek was written was modern paper, not parchment.

She turned a page and her mouth opened in awe. The page was covered in a beautiful illumination of Quetzalcoatl, the Aztec God of Life.

Lady Challis moved her fingers to the page but did not touch it. After Narmer's death and Amunet had taken her to the magical and beautiful land of South America, they had spent several years amongst the Aztecs, and she had watched stone masons carve such reliefs on new pyramids and effigies that adorned them. She dared to turn the page. Yes!

The language changed from Greek to Roman Latin, then back to ancient Nahuatl, the natural language of the Aztecs. Lady Challis looked up at Phaedra,

"If I continue in this book, what languages will I see?

"Quechuan, the language of the Andes, is still spoken today, but I learned it as a member of the Inca. Spanish, but not from the time of their rape of the continent. German. There are some Arabic, Japanese, Tibetan, Mongolian, Yiddish, and several languages native to Siberia." Phaedra paused.

"One of the intoxicating things about being immortal is being able to use it to span across knowledge. The tablet has images from caves and ancient rites as seen through the lens of time."

Phaedra rolled the tip of her cigar in the bowl, and, without looking at Lady Challis continued.

"It is about life, Mother Gaia, about our consciousness and our essential essence. It is about climbing the tree of life to the heavens and descending to the underworld. It helps me explore my spiritual awakening." Said Phaedra.

Lady Challis looked up sharply,

"Spiritual awakening. You mean you."

"We are all part of the genus Homo sapiens." Phaedra interrupted as she settled more comfortably in her chair; it seemed she was readying herself either for a debate or a nap.

"A genus is a rank in the biological classification and a taxonomy. It stands above species, and below families. A genus can include more than one species. When biologists talk about a genus, they mean one or more species of animals or plants that are closely related to each other. We are part of the genus Homo sapiens. Would you not say that?"

Lady Challis opened her mouth to speak and closed it as she considered the intellect behind the statement. It tripped off Phaedra's tongue so easily. She had considered the connection of humans and vampires. "Humans are not just food to be harvested, as Sophyra does." Mused Lady Challis.

"When was the last time you bit and killed a human?" Asked Phaedra.

Lady Challis opened her mouth to speak and said nothing, closing it slowly. Her mind raced, centuries pasted, a blur of images, thoughts, and deeds. Finally, it stopped.

A wood with dense green richness and undergrowth. North Amerika, maybe two decades after the first white settlers had landed. She looked down at her legs, thick long skirts, and a white cap on her head. She was leaning against a tree wiping blood from her mouth, her fangs moving back into their sockets. Her heart pounded from exertion and excitement so intense it was like an orgasm.

A dead native on the ground, a spilled basket of berries. The Indian decorated with feathers, a leather loin cloth, and moccasin shoes. His tomahawk with a shiny metal blade just a few feet from his hand. Her eyes were glued to the tell-tale puncture wounds on his neck.

He had surprised her; he was intent on carrying her off to his tribe to present to the chief. Oh, what a mistake that virile young man had made! She had killed him quickly and gorged on his blood. So delicious. So, invigorating. So natural for her. She quickly picked up the tomahawk, and took aim at the neck and started hacking at it. She needed to hide her fang marks.

"A long time ago... Another life."
"I thought so."

"You drink the blood of humans, don't you?"

"Yes, of course, all vampires do in one way or another. I prefer a nice crystal glass, but bare hands will do."

Phaedra puffed on her cigar and looked at the glowing embers she had created.

"Who do you think gave the Inca Qhapaq hucha, the practice of human sacrifice? If you had visited a temple when sacrifices were being made, you would have seen me filling a gourd with blood for later consumption. But we, like you, have never eaten humans, only Sophyra's kind do that."

Lady Challis slowly ran her fingers over the illumination of Quetzalcoatl, feeling the colours under her fingers.

"Are you saying you are spiritually aware?"

"Yes, and I see that in your future too. Elect-Si, you are aware through your shamanism. But you don't call it that; you enjoy confounding your guide." Phaedra pointed to a chair at the back of the room where they were sitting.

Elect-Si's head jerked in the direction Phaedra pointed. Sitting patiently, Elect-Si's guide sat cross-legged like a yogi, apparently in deep meditation, listening to everything being said.

"You can see my guide," Elect-Si blurted out!
"Of course."

Phaedra stopped sipping at her drink. She watched Lady Challis slowly and carefully leafing through her Bible.

"When you and Amunet were looking out over Machu Picchu, you saw a noble apparently kill another."

Lady Challis looked up sharply, "Yes."

"The noble on the ground was my human, Inca father, he adopted me, he hoped to marry me. But he had a disease; today we would call it cancer, a tumour in the brain that made it difficult for him to speak, and later in life, just when you saw him on the ground, he had problems walking."

"Go on."

"The noble standing over him was a close friend. They agreed my father would appear to pick a fight and that his old friend would kill him, which was easy, as my father could not swing his club. You saw the moment of my father's death."

"I am sorry."

"Thank you, but don't be. You had no way of knowing from your eagle's perch. Perhaps the message should be. Don't take things at face value."

"Is that a message about you? Your kind?"

"We are not so interested in the trappings of power. About being Pope, we are interested in stability and the growth of humankind. When humankind stands on the Moon, Mars … and any of the planets, we intend to be walking in their foot prints. We are happy with second place."

"But if first-place stumbles, you will be first." Interrupted Elect-Si.

Phaedra ignored the comment and continued staring at Lady Challis, who turned to look at her daughter.

"Not first, I think Phaedra would wait for another human to go first; she would be second and still the power behind the first place." Said Lady Challis

"Still, I want to ask, why the crosses?" Asked Lady Challis.

"Sacrifice. They do not remind me of Christ. They remind me to study life, existence, and the karma of all things and all lives. I am sure you are aware that as immortals, we move from existence to existence without passing through the evaluation of our Karma, even if we are aware of it. I find that each existence starts with influences of the previous one, like it or not."

Lady Challis drew inward; she became thoughtful. It had been centuries since she had last looked at her life, her existence, in a broad sweep, as Phaedra was prompting her to now. In a burst of energy, like a star exploding in the sky, she realized that each of her lives had been a continuation of the one she had just shrugged off like a snake shedding its skin.

In each life, she had unconsciously picked up where she had left off. No! it was more than picking up from where a previous life had ended; she saw how several times she had planned her next life to be an extension of the previous one.

Lady Challis refocused on Phaedra as she handed the bible back.

"You live eternity like a human soul, the same body, but with a different mind. Different intentions. Why kill Cassius?"

Phaedra shrugged.

"Perhaps you should think about all this under a full moon; there is one tonight.," she said as she reached for her glass and drained the amber liquid. She took one last puff at the cigar and stubbed it out.

"I killed Cassius. It was a gift from me to a lover; it was to save him from what was to come. Dorion mutilated and tortured him; she injected him with Sophyra enzymes. Within hours it would start eating him away from the inside."

As she started to lean forward to stand, Lady Challis spoke.

"Dinner tonight! We have to decide on what will happen to Sophyra!" said Lady Challis quickly. In her rush to speak, and set an agenda, an expectation for their next meeting, she realized Phaedra had been in control of the meeting all along.

"Dinner yes, but no more talk about Sophyra. Collect your thoughts, Challis. Tomorrow, we will decide on our approach to both Pope's. We want both eliminated."

Phaedra stood and looked down regally on Lady Challis, who was now sat back in her chair, her expression showing her mind slipping into deep thought.

Phaedra turned to walk out but stopped next to Elect-Si's chair. She smiled down at her. Suddenly, she reached out and, with a finger, lifted Elect-Si's chin, tilting her head backward. In a moment of speed and agility, she bent over and kissed Elect-Si on the lips. Straightening, Phaedra smiled again and moved to follow a servant to her suite.

23. A Full Moon

The full moon was bright and intense in the black night sky. Stars were out, galaxies and nebulae could be seen through the clear mountain air. She looked up, directly above her was the Milky Way. It hung there with the stars like pieces of an elaborate mobile over a child's crib.

She felt her hand being pulled very gently. She rolled over on the surface of the reflecting lake and looked into the eyes of her daughter.

"See. It is nice being out here, just floating on the lake, under the stars."

"Yes, I should have done it a long time ago. At the back of that sculpture, there is a place where we can get out of the water, sit, and talk; we must talk." Lady Challis's eyes closed as she felt the ripples of the warm lake water roll over her body.

Elect-Si squeezed the water from her long black hair as she looked at the reflection of the moon in the water.

"This is a nice comfy little space; I have not swum behind the sculpture before; I didn't know it was here."

Her mother was turned away from her. She was staring at the bright white snow of the Himalayas.

"The moon makes the snow so white. So pure. So, inviting and started to squeeze the water out of it. Will you take me some time and show me your Banjhakri?" "Of course. Are you thinking about what Phaedra said about your spiritual awakening?"

"This space was special, I guess … it still is. When the Maharaja and I lived here, servants would row out and leave wine and food here. We would swim out when the moon came up and fuck until dawn. When the sun was just about to come up, they would bring breakfast." Lady Challis paused.

"Those were amazing times. She turned back to rest against the smooth marble and looked up at the silvery moon.

"Elect-Si, don't waste your time on half lovers, don't choose half friends, don't entertain half art, don't choose half good wine. Don't live half a life…. Promise me that."

Elect-Si turned to look at her mother.

"I promise. Those words sounded very profound. Thoughts. Give me your thoughts."

Lady Challis used her hands to flick water droplets off her stomach and thighs.

"Phaedra was right about my spiritual awakening. Things have been changing inside of me since we arrived. There is more intensity to life; it is more vibrant and when, like now, all is at peace, I feel more in the moment. If that makes sense,"

"Why didn't you say anything? I'm your daughter. We sleep together, I … love you."

Lady Challis turned away from the moon and looked over at Elect-Si.

"I love you too! Very much. Very, very much. You were off in the Himalayas learning about your shamanic abilities and the rites and rituals of being so enlightened." Lady Challis paused as a fish surfaced a few feet away. It was jumping out of the water, trying to catch an insect. In the silence of the moment, the splash it made as it crashed into the water was surprising and took their attention away from the conversation.

"I had no idea."

"I did not want to distract you, confuse you." Lady Challis turned back to look at the reflection of the moon as it flowed like mercury over the ripples made by the fish.

"Existence seemed so simple. I am a vampire, I hunt, feast and move on, I kill when necessary. I am immortal." Lady Challis looked at her nails; the red varnish seemed to glow in the brightness of the moon light.

"I moved from existence to existence, outsmarting humans with ease. Then I fell in love with one."

"Narmer?"

"Yes." Lady Challis sighed.

"Humans have such short lives; they can only look beyond their time by hoping offspring will achieve greatness. They will start something, not knowing how it will be completed, they trust a later generation will have learned what to do."

"I gave our kind leadership, strength, unity, and faith in what they are. I helped them organize. I taught them how to use their power, not simply to be powerful. I helped them navigate through and around humans using my experience."

"Did you never suspect there were other kinds of vampires?"

"No."

"Not even when we were in South America?"

"No." Lady Challis looked at Elect-Si.

"First Sophyra, now Phaedra. It seems as though I have been living in a bubble where only our kind existed. Hearing Wellington tell his mother's childhood rhyme… The vampire in it, and the way he killed, could not have been made up; it was very detailed and accurate. The elves must have known."

"You could not…"

'Existence!' Interrupted, Lady Challis.

"Existence is starting to make sense, all of it. My awakening, I see the flow of time, like water from the high mountains to the sea, but I can see the snow in the high mountains was the sea until the sun heated the sea and it formed clouds. Then the wind blew the clouds to the mountains and rain fell as snow. It is a huge immense cycle of creation. I see the narrow gorges funnelling and making existence flow and rage over rocks under the surface. Rocks that are events that affect our lives but we never see them. I see waterfalls of time; I see it in still pools. I see the lazy spreading out over a flat valley. I see my life path."

"That is very wonderful," said Elect-Si quietly as she stared at her mother.

Lady Challis drew her knees-up in front of her and hugged them.

"There is a fourth kind of vampire. Can you see that?"

Elect-Si ran her hand over the smooth marble and brushed some water back into the lake.

"Tell me."

"It's you. You are the fourth kind of vampire that will walk this earth." Lady Challis turned to look at her daughter and rested her cheek on her knees.

"You can see that, can't you?"

Elect-Si felt strength and power well up inside of her. Something that had been there for a while now, ever since she visited the Underworld. It felt like energy that rotated, like the protective search light from a light house on a dark and stormy night. Bright and intense one moment then dark and brooding. Many sailors see the beacon of a light house as bright and wonderful and saving them from the rocks, then it is dark and absent only to reappear again. Elect-Si now saw the darkness as a different form of light. The Ying and Yang in her were starting to come to life. It was no longer a representation of good and evil; it was a representation of two types of good.

"Yes, mother, I can."

"You did not have fangs when I purged the Count's venom from you. You had been his for long enough for them to start to form. After I bit you, you had them within days." She paused.

"There has never been a shaman vampire, a white shaman who visits other realms."

"You have been taking to Gwen."

"Yes, in great, great, great detail. Everything she knows, and everything she can remember." Lady Challis stopped speaking and her eyes closed. Sounds of the night animals and fish splashing on the surface were all they heard.

"When you were decimating Aldeburgh, did you feed?"

"Only vampires. I only fed on other vampires." Elect-Si felt a meaning in the question, but decided to wait for her mother to voice her thoughts. Above her, the edge of thin, high cirrus clouds covered the moon and the powerful glow of that white disk lit up the clouds like some magical imperial light.

"They became so devoted to me, it … they were quite amazing."

"You will have to bit a human. You know that, don't you?"

"Why must I do that?"

"Baby, in all the centuries you have been my daughter, you have bitten fewer beings than some vampires bite in a day. When you bit those vampires, did you sense anything?"

Elect-Si rubbed her eyes.

"I could sense the enzymes of the one who made them a vampire. It was like pressure on my fangs, trying to block the duct in my fangs. In some, the pressure was weak; in others it was much stronger and potent. But whatever the feeling, I just brushed it aside and injected my own." She turned to look at her mother.

"Is that how it was when you made me your daughter?"

"Something like that. I needed to put you through all those trials, the tests, to make sure you were cleansed. It seems you can achieve the same all the terror you suffered with me."

Elect-Si looked at the now clear moon, bright and round and marked by meteors and other celestial bodies that had crashed into it. She studied its surface, her mind blank of anything she should say next until a few words started to shine on what she was looking at.

"Thank you for biting me. Thank you for being my mother."

"You are very welcome. Tell me, how did the vampires you bit react?"

Elect-Si's mind skipped back to those short few months when you culled the covens and secured their unswerving allegiance.

"A couple died, writhing on the ground in front of me. Oddly, they were completely silent in their agonies. They did not shout or scream." Elect-Si paused.

"I cut one open, all of their organs had turned black, some appeared burned and charred. The rest, not much suffering." She turned to look at her mother,

"We have to decide how I am going to bite Sophyra?"

"Phaedra wants her dead. What are you getting at?" Asked Lady Challis.

"If Sophyra is like the vampires in Aldeburgh, after they are bitten, if they do not die, they follow my instructions without question. If we kill her, we have to find another candidate for Pope. Are you against being pope now?" Asked Elect-Si.

'Oh, I am not to be Pope. Not now. I thought of you, but I think you would be better without the burden and restrictions. There is one thing you have not done that is crucial. You have not died and moved on to another existence. Doing that as Pope would be very testing, something you do not need for the first time."

"I think I could handle it..." murmured Elect-Si.

Lady Challis extended her legs and tilted her head back.

"It is not just the fake death. It is..." she stopped speaking for a moment.

"It is how you reinvent myself; it is what you create for the new you. In Egypt I allowed myself to be knocked into the Nile and appeared to drown. As I floated down the river, there was a feeling of luxury. I had time to see and think. I planned it to be brighter, wiser, purer, and more powerful me than before."

Her mother stopped for a moment.

"Power, not as a noble person, but within myself. My spirit, my soul. I think that is where I first sensed my awakening." Lady Challis let out a deep sigh.

"But like humans who get distracted by the pressures of their short lives, I got distracted too, only I was distracted for millennia." She turned a hard stare at her daughter.

"Immortality will do that to you. Make sure it doesn't happen to you. I drifted into some reeds and sat there until my clothes dried. I let my royal robes downstream and away from me, and I put on those of a serving woman. A serving woman was what I was when I stood up." Lady Challis folded her hands in her lap.

"When I got out of the reeds, Narmer was still pharaoh, he was getting married to another woman and everyone was celebrating. Nothing had changed. When I spoke, people challenged me and shouted at me. Things they would not have dared to do just hours before. Food was coarse, basic, and limited. It had no spices, no richness and no taste. It filled the belly, that was all. There was no wine." Lady Challis reached out a hand and splashed some still water from the marble bench they were sitting on.

"In the human world, you are dead, gone, never to return. As an immortal moving to a new existence, you can never contact any human you once knew. If you meet them accidentally, you cannot recognize them. In that there is sadness, great sadness sometimes. Better to do it quietly."

Elect-Si could feel the heaviness in her mother's voice. She was not sure how to respond so she kept quiet.

Lady Challis moved to run her fingers through her now dry hair.
"Sophyra sought the role and the title; let her keep it but you must control her."

"What about the other pope?"

"Phaedra can deal with him."

Lady Challis moved to the edge of the bench and slowly slipped into the water. She turned to look at Elect-Si as she floated on the silvery water.

"Come on. The sun is already up. We should be back at the palace to deliver our strategy to Phaedra."

24.   What Do You Tell Phaedra?

Elect-Si flipped her hand mirror around to the side that magnified her face. Briskly, her tweezers moved across her face, plucking a few last stray hairs from her eyebrows. She flipped the mirror back to the other side and was pleased with the final results. As she moved the mirror around to get a better look at her face, a human form shivered in the background and then was gone.

Her fangs falling into place and her sharp vampire eyes and ears at full intensity, she looked for a threat that had somehow gotten into her suite. Her heart raced and her breathing was deep, filling her blood with oxygen to feed the intense reaction in her muscles as she prepared to fight.

"What the fuck are you doing?" her eyes landed on her guide sitting now on the end of her bed.

"Hi Elect-Si. It's only me!" He waved a hand and smiled like a child who has been caught with his hand in the cookie jar and was now trying to be innocent and mischievous at the same time.

"How long have you been there?"

"Let's see." He rested his chin on his hand and adopted a thoughtful expression.

"Since Lady Challis bit you. Yes. That would be right," he paused and looked out of the window.

"I have been with you since birth and your human birth, but I wasn't active. You had other guides that dominated then. It was Lady Challis. The moment she bit you, everything changed." His look gave her the feeling she had been born a second time, and in that moment the previous version of herself had died. When your mother bit you, a new being came into the world."

Elect-Si opened her mouth to speak but her guide held up a finger to stop her.

"When Lady Challis bit you, that is I came to guide you."

"Why is this important?"

"Because you are planning to do the same to Sophyra. You are going to become her mother." He nodded with finality and slipped off the bed. He walked slowly to sit at the chair beside Elect-Si's makeup table.

"The fuck I am!" She reached for the switch to turn off the intense makeup lights so she could see him more clearly.

Her guide shook his head and frowned.

"You do understand what your mother did to you… You are as loyal and close to her as you could ever be. You are more to her than you were to your human mother while you were human." He shook his head and looked towards the open doors of the suite and the balcony.

"I was sitting next to you on the bench this morning. When you and your mother plotted to bite and control Sophyra."

"You saw us naked, on the bench?"

"I see, hear, smell, and since your touch in every moment of your existence."

"Really, everything?"

"There are times when I encourage you to do things, to get the most you can out of an experience. That little voice in your head, that is me." He smiled.

"You have some wonderful thoughts all on your own!" He looked away and then snapped his attention back to her.

"Things are changing between us, you can feel them, can't you?"

"I guess you can also stop me from doing things?"

"Yes, that is true."

Elect-Si toyed with the tweezers she had just used. Her mind moved through her thoughts and memories. Finally, she found one that was slightly out of place. Before Petr went on the raid with Miray, there had been an evening when she wanted to sleep with him. There seemed to be a feeling or romance about it. A dreamy Hollywood war movie feeling. A woman sleeping with her man before he went off to war, partly for the shared memories each of them would carry for the rest of their lives. Party, because of the possibility of getting pregnant and having a child to remember the father by.

It had not worked out. She had gone for a long flight into the Himalayas. She wanted to clear her mind before bedding Petr. She had landed on a cliff edge and sat hugging her knees as she considered her motives for doing what she planned. She knew she didn't want to have a child. Immortality has its benefits. She could have a child at any time between now and the end of time.

Petr was interesting to her in a lustful way, not as a parent of her child. She had bitten him, saved his life and as they say, sired him. That created a certain primal connection.

She had decided it was lust making her want him physically. Pure and simple, animal lust.

As she was about to stand and extend her wings. She became entranced by some Yeti foraging for food. She watched and devoured their movements and their sounds; she could feel their essence. So moving, so intelligent, so powerful and so gentle.

It was late when she had returned. Petr had left early with Miray and the assault team. When she learned that she knew she would never see him again and never have the opportunity to enjoy him.

She dropped the tweezers, which made a metallic rattling sound on the marble top of her makeup table.

"The Yeti. They were your idea?"
"No. It was the turn you made into their valley instead of coming straight home. I had no idea they were there."

"I chose that turn … or, did you?"

He frowned, "Maybe you did, maybe not."

"Well, no matter now, he is dead. No sense in worrying about him."

He stared at her.

"You have a decision to make about Sophyra. What you and your mother tell Phaedra can't be what you discussed on the bench."

"What do you mean? You are supposed to be a guide, not giving instructions. What happened to free will? I am supposed to make my own decisions and you guide me."

"My guidance is that you do not tell Phaedra what you and your mother spoke about." He tapped his finger on the marble top and to Elect-Si it seemed to make a distinct sound, the tapping of a finger nail her ears could hear.

"I can hear you tap the table top…"

"Yes, wonderful, isn't it? Things are changing, as I said. The veil between the human physical world and the spirit world you know as a shaman is becoming thinner. Soon it won't be there."

"Is that good?"

"For us, you and me, yes. But it means you will be The Gatekeeper between the different realms of existence." He looked at her strangely.

"You were given such a powerful Toli for a reason." He searched her eyes with his.

"You are immortal. When the veil drops, it will never be raised again. When you look back from the end of time, we will see the worlds have never merged, that you kept them separate. You judged those who tried to cross over and above all, you enforced your judgment. Then we will turn around and carry on…"

"When the shaman gave me this Toli, she never said anything about this. You. You never said anything!" said Elect-Si leaning forward.

"That is true." He smiled. "Now, about Phaedra."

"Hold on, you can't just skip over this!" Said Elect-Si firmly, rapping on the table with her fist.

Her guide frowned.

"We, yes, you and I can skip over this. I will be with you every step of the way; I will never leave your side. And, by the way, it is all your angels and guides who will be with you. We are all in this together. You will not be, and never will be, alone."

"Then take this Toli off, give it to someone else."

"Can't do that, no one can. Besides, you are immortal. An immortal should wear it. When you first visited the other realms, you knew nothing about Toli and ritual things, yet you did not hesitate to take action; you did not ask about consequences; your actions were astonishing to us. What you have done since protected by the Toli has been overwhelming."

"What if I stop astounding you?"

"You can't; it is in your nature to surprise. You are a living Ying and Yang. Whoever looks at you, whichever facet they choose, white or black, they will see the essence of the opposite in you. You really are unique." He sighed.

"What?'

Her guide was silent for several moments then he turned to her.

"When you journeyed to the Underworld to retrieve the soul fragment, many of your guides said that is all you would do. I said no, you would amaze us. You shook us to the core. Even I was shaken. But I was happy to be surprised. You dismembered the black shaman but did not kill him. You bound him to the ground, to the earth, and left him guarded by trees. Trees that will live for eternity because of you. You burned parts of his body in a tower of the purest, pure white light." He leaned forward for emphasis.

"That tower of light was seen everywhere in the Underworld. Not just where you stood." He leaned further forward.

"Everywhere," his eyes narrowed, "and we all know you."

"To me, what I did is what I knew I had to do."

"That is what shakes us. Another might say, I will go and do this because I have an unassailable Toli of such power nothing can harm me. Not you. You say, I will go and do this or that because that is what needs to be done, this is what is right to do, oh, and by the way, I am protected by something beyond all realms. Think back, the Black Shaman had to remind you how you are protected. Until he spoke, you had never thought of it."

A long moment of silence followed. Idly, Elect-Si pushed the tweezers around the table top.

"OK, let me know when the veil drops." She met the gaze of her guide.

"Now, to Phaedra."

25.   What to Say Now

Elect-Si looked down at the translucent Fang lying on a bed of medical gel. This was such a small and yet powerful part of her. Now that it was separated from her body, the sense of intimacy and loss grew and grew. This was more than sex; it was more than having a baby. The Fang could be replaced; indeed, her body was already growing a new one but this part of her had been with her since just after her mother had bitten her. In all the centuries, she had never broken a fang or damaged one. Now, she had purposefully broken one.

She consoled herself with the fact fangs are made to break off. When a food source struggles while being bitten, fangs can and do separate to preserve vampires and they are made to grow back quickly.

Her tongue touched the root of the fang and could feel it had already healed over. An essential roughness had formed to protect the new Fang as it grew.

She moved the box to better display a hint of the golden liquid inside the fang.

"That is more than enough," said Phaedra.

"Break that bitches' skin with the tip, and the fang will automatically inject it."

"How long until you have control of her?" Asked Phaedra as she moved the container around to let sunlight catch the fang shell and liquid inside it.
"Less than a minute."

"That quick!"

Elect-Si shrugged. She looked across the room at her guide sitting cross-legged like a yogi on a comfortable cushion.

"I don't eat human flesh; none of my kind do. Sophyra will vomit every bite of human flesh in her system after it takes effect. Be prepared." Elect-Si closed the lid and momentarily hesitated to hand over the nondescript medical container.

She was giving away a part of herself but was consoled by thinking of how much they would be gaining.

Elect-Si moved to the humidor and lifted the lid. She selected a rare Cuban cigar. She held it up to show Phaedra, who nodded that she would like one too.

Elect-Si carefully trimmed the ends with her cigar cutter. She lifted her lighter to the tip so that Phaedra could draw on the cigar and pull the flame into the tip and inhale.

Phaedra nodded her thanks and moved away to the verandah railing. As she puffed on the cigar, she looked out over the lake.

"Excuse me Elect-Si, is now a good time for me to join the meeting?"

Phaedra whirled around at the unknown voice. In spite of the cigar smoke, her nose visibly twitched and inhaled. "I thought we were all vampires here." She pointed at Manuel.

"He is human."

Elect-Si turned to look at Manuel,

"Yes, I suppose you are human, aren't you?"

Manuel nodded. And she smiled.

"I had the incredible pleasure of being a husband to one of your kind," he pointed at Phaedra.

"Her name was Ximena. Her loss was beyond what I could bear for months. I journeyed for an audience with Lady Challis and came away with admiration for her and all that she stood for. I am as loyal to her as any vampire of her kind, and that loyalty extends to her daughter, Elect-Si."

Phaedra glared at him.

"You say you were married to one of my kind? I do not understand why you are still human. She should have scratched you often."

Manuel held out his hands so showed he had no finger nails.

"I could never be one of your kind; I cannot scratch. I cannot inject enzymes."
Phaedra blinked as she looked at his fingers.

"She should have scratched you and made you one of us anyway."

Manuel opened the leather case containing his tablet.

"The war will have to stop; weapons and supplies shipped to the army will have to be scaled back quickly, then end up. Shipments of human meat products will have to end." He looked at Phaedra.

"Shipments of uranium will be diverted and then stopped. Repatriation of soldiers for training as priests, that needs some work. Have I missed anything?"

Phaedra studied Manuel cautiously.

"No, those are the major pieces on the chess board."

"I have been auditing shipments into and out of the region. And found this."

Phaedra exhaled and studied Elect-Si and Manuel.

"What do you think he has found?" asked Phaedra to Elect-Si.

"Direct your question to Manuel, not me." Replied Elect-Si as she moved to sit on an ottoman close to where her guide was sitting.

Phaedra remained unmoved for several minutes, weighing her options at what might be described on Manuel's tablet. Finally, in a huff and shaking over shoulders, she moved to a table to look at the tablet. She scrolled up and down the inventory worksheet.

Elect-Si winked at Manuel as Phaedra walked back to the verandah railing.

"Manuel, Phaedra is not paying you any compliments on your audit. Perhaps you can tell us what you have discovered."

Manuel picked up his tablet and simply held it to his side. He did not need to look at it.

"Two months after the war began, shipments of refined gold started being smuggled to South Amerika. It is now consistently between seventy-five and one hundred tons each month. Six months after the gold shipments began, diamonds and sapphires started shipping to the same destinations. The stones are of the highest quality. There is between one third and a half of a ton each month. Offshore dredges have started dragging the sea floor. They are vacuuming up between one and two tons of low-quality diamonds for industrial purposes." He spoke.

"These are being smuggled in tin cans used for canned fruit and beans."

Phaedra slapped the marble railing top several times with the palm of her right hand.

"You do your job too well." She scowled and turned to face Elect-Si and Manuel.

"A little savings account for my kind. We can agree it will continue until the end of the war." She looked at Elect-Si, who was now emulating her guide by sitting cross-legged on a large cushion.

Elect-Si slowly opened her eyes and stood up. She held her free hand under her cigar as ash dropped from it, she caught it and dropped it in a convenient ash tray.

"We can if twenty percent of everything comes to us. We need a savings account as well."

Phaedra groaned out loud and flicked ash from her cigar on to the floor.

"We can agree." She pouted at Manuel.

"You can make that happen, I suppose?"

"Gladly." Replied Manuel, offering a small formal bow.

"I will leave for home tonight." She picked up the container with Elect-Si's fang and tapped it with her finger nail.

"You will hear from me." She turned and left the room.

"Make sure our twenty percent ships separately from our own take from the war."

"Of course. Shipments to them have declined recently, apparently due to setbacks in the war, or so they believe. But really, we are already skimming from their shipments."

Elect-Si grinned broadly.

"Mother said you were good. I have some other projects we can work on together. I will talk to Mother about us doing so." She studied his face; she liked it.

26.   The Yeti Understand

"Crap! Crap! Crap!"

Elect-Si breathed heavily as she ran through the water dripping off the rocks above her. The cold Himalayan air surged into her lungs. Her fists pumped hard to drive the air in and out of her body. Her heart raced in a way it had not done for centuries. The power in her legs seemed to be at their limit. The great strides of the Yeti above and behind her were eroding the lead her fast-moving legs had given her.

Above, she could hear the heavy steps of Yeti; behind her, the rock scree moved violently under the weight of others. Great screams of rage and anger, followed by primal, guttural growls, filled the still night air.

Rocks the size of grapefruit whistled past her. Some into the large boulders to her right smashed into pieces from the violence of the impact.

She abruptly moved sideways, leaping on to a huge flat rock that had broken off the cliff above her. It must be 400 to 500 yards long, she estimated. Under the full moon, she could see the surface was slick with water spilling on to it from a melting glacier up the valley.

Her boots had no traction on the glazed surface and she found herself hunched into the stance she used on her antique snowboard. For a moment, the chase had become exhilarating and exciting. The familiarity of the position and a fleeting memory of snowboarding down the Matterhorn one dark night when no one was watching filled her mind and helped her refine her balance. It allowed her a moment to look back.

Five large yetis raged and flung their arms in the air on the cliff above. Mouths open, the sound of their anger filled the valley.

Then her eyes looked at the huge slab she was on. One Yeti, perhaps younger and more athletic, had managed to follow her on to it but had lost its footing. It was on its back, arms, and legs waving wildly as it tried to roll over to stand.

The sound of rushing water ahead brought Elect-Si's attention back to what was to come. The water sounded immense. Her acute vampire vision allowed her to make out a fast-moving mountain river.

Her wings emerged.

She squatted lower on the rock and sprang into the air. She felt Amunet deliver a powerful gust that took her twenty feet into the air on one beat of her wings.

Behind her, a bellow of rage made her turn to look at the Yeti who had chased her on to the rock. He was now uncontrollably sliding on the slope towards its end; the end would dump it into the river and a waterfall further down. He waved his arms in rage as he looked up at her escaping his retribution.

Elect-Si pirouetted on her right wing and came in behind the young Yeti. He tried to turn to grasp her but she was too quick for it. Her fingers grabbed the thick matted fur behind its neck and her wings beat furiously with deep power.

Her mind focused on the tops of the trees she had pulled back and let go when she first learned to fly at the mansion. She heaved and pulsed her wings powerfully. She felt Amunet thicken the air under them, giving her the purchase; she needed to lift the great beast onto the tips of its toes. Just enough to allow her to move it to the side of the rock where it could walk. She grunted with the effort, which made the Yeti turn its great head and look up at her. Their eyes met; for a moment there was silence, as the Yeti seemed to understand. This running, flying creature was saving it. It allowed her to take it over to the edge and drop it on a scree slope.

She hovered for a moment as the Yeti got to its knees.

"Higher…. Higher. You need to be higher." She heard Amunet whisper.

Elect-Si put several powerful beats into her wings to raise her thirty or forty feet into the air. As she continued to look down, the Yeti stood but turned quickly, picking up a rock, which it unleashed at her. It skimmed past her right leg.

The missed throw brought bellows of rage and waving of arms and fists in her direction.

Elect-Si felt the air thicken noticeably and her wing beats to hover much higher … and higher. With one last look at the Yeti on the cliff, she turned and allowed her wings and Amunet to lift her higher and higher until she disappeared over the mountains at the edge of the valley.

She turned in the direction of the Palace and set a fast pace for her wings.

27.　Gwendoline's Cane

Elect-Si rolled over in bed and tried to go back to sleep but was abruptly prodded in the small of her back by something hard and small. She pulled the sheets up around her as she rolled over to see what it was.

She exhaled an overly large and dramatic sigh. It was Gwendoline's cane. It hovered by the side of her bed as if asking the question.

"When are you getting out of bed, lazy girl?"

She closed her eyes and threw the sheets back. The cane moved backward a few feet to give her space to get out of bed and put on a robe. By the large open verandah doors, she could see the long white hair of Gwendoline as she read her tablet.

"Did you get the question?" Asked Gwendoline.

Elect-Si did not answer. She looked into the corner of the room where her own cane hovered.

"Aren't you supposed to protect me from things like that?" she said pointing to Gwendoline's cane. The reaction was immediate and unexpected. Her own cane shot across the room, knocking Gwendoline's proxy out of the way.

From the verandah, a peal of laughter erupted and a slender hand appeared, beckoning her cane back to her side.
Elect-Si took hold of her cane. And walked somewhat tiredly to Gwendoline.

"You could have ordered breakfast!" she exclaimed.

"Lunch, I should have ordered lunch! It's midday." She looked at Elect-Si's cane.

"Why are you here?" Asked Elect-Si sitting down and resting her hands and chin on the handle of her cane.

"In the old days, that cane would have been called your staff, shaman. Take it everywhere you go. I mean everywhere. There is a very powerful and protective spirit in it. It must protect you at all times. My proxy should not have gotten close to you." She paused, staring at Elect-Si's cane.

"It loves you very much. You, we, may call our staff a cane today, but really, it is your shaman's staff." Her gaze moved up to Elect-Si's eyes.

"It may stop you doing stupid things like scaring the Yeti."

Elect-Si studied the handle on her cane. A tingling sensation started across her head and expanded down into neck and shoulders, then her entire body. A field of wheat shimmered and became solid. She could feel the warm sun-drenched soil under her bare feet. To her left a playful, happy voice called her name. She turned in its direction; Emma was running to greet her.

"It is so good to see you!" exclaimed Emma. The girl waved her arms in the air.

"See! I still have both arms. Thanks to you, I can play with the other children and have fun just as they do." Emma held out both hands to Elect-Si.

Elect-Si slipped her hands into Emma's and drew the girl to her and hugged warmly for a long time.

"I am so glad to see you, Emma. I am glad that you can run and play like the others. It sounds as though you have made some new friends?"

"Yes, many new friends," gushed Emma staring at Elect-Si quizzically.

"She has not realized who you are." Said a male voice from behind Elect-Si.

Elect-Si took a quick step to one side and whirled around. Behind her, chewing on a stalk of grass was her guide. He was not looking at Elect-Si, he was looking at Emma. He smiled.

"Shall we tell her?"

Emma held on to one of Elect-Si's hands.

"Yes, I think we should."

"Tell me what?" Blurted out Elect-Si.

"Emma's spirit is in your cane … your shaman's staff." He waited for Elect-Si to react, but receiving nothing but a blank stare, he continued.

"Gwendoline is right, your cane should bn call a Shaman's staff. Well in the old days, in a few places, it still is. But plodding around with a staff six feet tall like Gandalf would be stupid today. You are contemporary with the world around you even if the cane is somewhat elaborate."

Elect-Si looked down at Emma, who smiled up at her.

"She is not sure…"

"Emma's spirit will protect and guide you through the cane; it allows Emma into the physical world," Elect-Si looked down at Emma's small hand in hers.

"Elect-Si, you may see Emma as a child, a small hand in yours. But I see a spirit, a soul of enormous power, age, and wisdom that I cannot measure it. She too was a White Shaman, as you are. She was a very powerful one. She left the physical world over ten thousand years ago. She has been waiting for you all that time."

"Go on, tell me everything."

"Emma's arm was cut off by a warlord she confronted when she was a physical being. He had pledged himself to the power of a Black Shaman in his tribe. He vowed to crush her White Shamanism and all white shamans in his lands."
"Go on, tell me everything."

Her guide looked at Emma, who nodded.

"The Black Shaman in the warlord's tribe cursed Emma. She was never to have her arm back, and never to play with other children. For ten thousand years, she has waited for you to come and undo the curse and restore her arm."

Elect-Si looked down at the sweet young face looking up at her and the hand in hers. She knelt down and hugged Emma, who threw her arms around Elect-Si's neck.

"You have been waiting that long for me!"

Emma smiled and nodded.

Elect-Si slowly stood, still holding Emma's hand.

"I don't recall undoing any curse."

Her guide took another stalk of wheat and studied the full heavy head of grain.

"That is another of your, shall we call them superpowers." Emma, who giggled.

"You undid the curse by simply ignoring it. It meant nothing to you. Then you healed Emma by giving her back her arm. Then she could play with the others."

Elect-Si looked down at Emma.
"Could no one help you in all that time?"

Emma frowned.

"Hundreds tried but all failed. They allowed the curse to prevent them. They could sense it and stopped. I just had to be patient until you came."

Elect-Si put her arms around Emma and simply picked her up like a mother picking up a young child who made the girl giggle as Elect-Si got the girl comfortable on her hip. She turned to her guide, who had an expression of surprise and shock on his face.

"Am I not supposed to pick Emma up like this? Get used to it. This is reality for us. Emma and I will be together for longer than eternity!"

"Is that a curse? Curses can be good and bad."

"It is reality. When I turn and look over my shoulder to the end of time, and continue on." Elect-Si paused.

"No! It is not I; it is we. We will be together looking back at the end of time. We will be together as we continue on we will be inseparable."

Emma hugged Elect-Si's neck tightly, whispering into her ear.

Elect-Si started to feel the earth under her feet become cooler, the soil, the ground became harder, slowly the field of wheat and her guide lost focus. They drifted in her consciousness and were gone. Her eyes are now focused on the marble floor and her toes. She hugged her cane to her chest, the handle snugged up tight to the side of her head and her ear. It vibrated with a satisfying softness. She kissed the handle and felt the vibrations intensify and then die away.

She stood up.

She looked at Gwendoline, who had a mixture of a smile and quizzical look om her face.

"Did you meet the spirit in your staff? I mean cane?"

"Yes"

Gwendoline took hold of her cane and slowly stood up. She started to walk away and then stopped. Half turning, she looked back over her shoulder,

"We are so fucked…"

28.   A Queen Awakens

Phaedra held out the small medical box to the old gardener. He took with soil-stained hands. And slowly rotated it between his fingers.

"It looks so small."

"Open it if you wish."

The gardener ran a dirty, cracked, finger nail along the edge, stopping to rest it on the magnetic clasp.

"No. My hands are dirty from the garden. Are you sure this is enough for what we wish to achieve?"

"Yes. But…" Phaedra hesitated.

"We must alter our plans." Phaedra threw back her head and ran her fingers through her long hair.

The gardener held out the medical box for her to take back.

"I can see that." He paused and looked at her admiringly,

"I am glad you made the decision by yourself. You have finally stepped into your power." He pursed his lips as he sensed things slipping away from him.

"You will be a great queen for our kind."

Phaedra slowly slipped the box into a hidden space in her robes.

"All I ever wanted to do was to have your baby's father." She met his old eyes with a direct, powerful stare.

"Our kind needs someone with the grace, ruthlessness, cunning, and stature of Challis, Elect-Si, and Sophyra." He tilted his head slightly as if listening.

"It was your idea to exploit the fanged one's plan to replace Sophyra." He straightened his neck and looked up at the clear night sky and the stars overhead, and nodded affirmatively as if coming to a decision. He looked at Phaedra for a long moment.

"Control of Sophyra is better than killing her. I can see that." A rumbling cough in his chest started and then did not appear on his lips.

"You cannot have my baby." He held up his hand quickly to stop any words of protest.

"That part of our plan must change. You can see that, can't you?"

Phaedra rubbed her eyes and covered her mouth as if preventing herself from throwing up. Behind her hand, she silently whispered the words.

"Thank You!"

"Yes. Father." She hesitated.
"Have a baby with someone of the fanged genre, someone close to Elect-Si. No child with any one of Sophyra's kind. Never… Never. Remember, you are to stand as our Queen. You must never touch the cock of one of her kind. You are not a whore." He straightened, throwing back his shoulders, and filling his chest with air and pride.

"The baby may be difficult for you. The vampire genres have always been separated for so long. The baby will be the first crossing … the first merging." He frowned and closed his eyes.

"Your child will be the foundation of the fourth genre of vampire and with its birth, the holy quadripartite will be complete." His voice took on a thickness, a reverent tone of a priest as he spoke the word.

"With you as its Mother and our Queen, we will subjugate the other species."

Phaedra nodded and lowered her eyes to the old man's chest. The dirt and sweat stained, once white shirt, were made from the finest Egyptian cotton. The buttons still revealed the shine of Mother-of-Pearl. Her mind dwelled on what sort of man would use such a fine garment for their daily manual labour.

"I am strong, father."

"I know. Now go. You must find a way to deliver that Fang to Sophyra and bury it in her festering body. Then, you must find a fanged one close to Elect-Si to impregnate you." With those words, he took out a small envelope, the same as the others he had given Phaedra over the months, and ripped the end off. He turned the envelope over and tipped the contents onto the ground.

"There will be no more of this." He crushed the paper in his hands and threw it away. With his heavy work boot, he flipped small amounts of soil over the place where the contents of the envelope had fallen, and packed it all down.

Phaedra slowly started to turn away to go back inside.

"What will happen to the one we planned to replace Sophyra?"

"Why do you ask?"

"I am Queen, I need control."

A smile started to cross the old man's lips; he was enjoying seeing her become the role planned for her.

"What do you want done?"

Phaedra paused for a moment, then she held out her hand.

"You have something for me."

The old man raised an eyebrow and reached into a pocket and brought out a garotte.

"I almost forgot."

"No. You did not forget," said Phaedra as she took it.

"Send him to my chambers tonight." She held up the garotte and looked from it to the old man.

"Tomorrow, have my rooms cleaned while I supervise dawn services." She turned and strode purposefully to the entrance and disappeared inside.

29.   A Gift is Received

Pope Sophyra smiled at the gold service platter that had been placed at the end of the table.

"I love gifts!" her voice almost let out an anticipatory giggle as she stepped forward to look at the gold, jewel box on its velvet cushion.

She prodded the cushion with her finger, moving it so it was perfectly aligned with the gold serving platter rim. She reached for and sipped from her glass of blood.

Her hands started to reach for the box, but diverted to a shinning crystal bowl of cheek meat, flesh cut from human babies culled shortly after birth. She lifted the silver serving fork and twirled it between her fingers. She looked at Phaedra.

"I cannot tell you how grateful I am that you stepped up to the fill the void left by Dorion. She was a very sad loss. I cried when I heard the news."

Phaedra smiled thinly, according to the priests present in the room when the news was delivered, Pope Sophyra had sniffed for maybe ten seconds and then moved the meeting on to the next subject.

Phaedra watched in hidden trepidation as Pope Sophyra moved to the jewel box. All of her hopes and dreams, and those of her kind had come down to the contents of the box.

Pope Sophyra forked two cheeks into her mouth and chewed as her attention turned back to the jewel box.

"Can I open it?" her voice taking on the tone of a child sitting under a richly laden tree at Christmas.

Phaedra smiled warmly and nodded.

Sophyra forked another cheek into her mouth and learned forward to insert the fork prongs into the gap between the two halves of the box. She twisted the fork and the lid opened slowly exposing an antique writing instrument on its satin pillow.

"I hope you like it; I know how much you enjoy using antique writing instruments and paper."

Without picking up the pen, Pope Sophyra picked up the box and turned it around in her hands, studying the pen.

"It is what they call a roller ball. Inside the pen is a metal container. On one end is a very small, very finely made metal ball. It fits very tightly but not so securely the ball cannot roll, picking up ink from inside a tube, and smearing it on paper as your hand moves the pen."

Phaedra smiled, but Pope Sophyra was not looking at her. She was fascinated by her gift.

"I managed to secure some ink containers in different colours, and I found an antique artisan who can manufacture more if you need them."

"Of course, I will need them!" exclaimed Pope Sophyra. She turned to look at Phaedra;

"I will use it every day." She reached into the box and picked up the pen.

"See, this end is a plunger; you press down on it to extend the end of the end for writing." Pope Sophyra rested her thumb on the plunger as she admired the fine engraving on the pen. On the other hand, she held over the writing end. She pressed down hard.

Phaedra reached into the space between her breasts in the low-cut front of her vestments. Her thumb rested on a garotte and slipped it into the palm of her hand, concealing it as she moved closer to Pope Sophyra.

Pope Sophyra gasped. She slowly and carefully put the pen back on the satin pillow it had rested on. She looked at her thumb; a small ball of blood was forming where it had been pricked by something sharp in the pen. Now she was gasping for air, her chest heaved and her breasts leaped free from her bustier. Her throat seemed to be alive with small animals, as it visibly constricted and then released as the muscles in it contorted.

The heavy gold crucifix swung back and forth, touching her nipples as if blessing them.

Pope Sophyra grasped the edge of the mahogany table.

Phaedra moved quickly; she kicked, catching Pope Sophyra's fingers against the table and breaking them before they could touch the alarm hidden underneath the edge. Then she slammed her fist between Pope Sophyra's breasts, sending her reeling backward away from the table into another chair.

Pope Sophyra stared at Phaedra, her eyes unfocused, the pupils dilated. Then she closed her eyes as she started to snort and sneeze violently.

Phaedra covered her mouth to stop from laughing. The Pope farted loudly and without any apparent end. As the sounds stopped, she started dry heaving and rolling from side to side in the spacious chair. As she rolled, thick white mucous liquid oozed from her mouth. What happened next sent Phaedra several steps backward. Like a baby vomiting up its food, Pope Sophyra started to violently project her vomit across the floor, the table and all over herself.

Phaedra moved behind the Pope. Pope Sophyra seemed oblivious to anything happening around her. Phaedra picked up the gold platter to make sure it did not get splattered with projectile vomit. She looked at the pen's plunger and the small translucent tip of Elect-Si's fang sticking out.

"Still a fair amount left, let's empty it, let's make sure." She said to herself.

She pulled at one of Pope Sophyra's broken fingers and jabbed it violently with the fang. A small ball of blood appeared after she took the plunger away from the flesh. Phaedra drove the fang into the finger again, and again. The reaction was immediate and violent. Pope Sophyra arched her back and her head shot forward, mouth open wide, projectile vomit spewed forward, knocking over anything in its path.

Phaedra reached into her vestments and took out a silk handkerchief. Inside was an identical pen; she reached down and pulled at Pope Sophyra's other hand and manipulated the fingers to leave finger prints where the pen would normally be held. Carefully she switched the pens.

She wiped the small balls of dried blood from the Pope's fingers.

She studied the scene for a long moment to make sure there was nothing she had missed.

Phaedra slipped out her smartphone and took pictures and video of the scene and the Pope lying in the chair amidst the solids of her vomit.

She reached under the table for the alert button and pressed it.

In what seemed like minutes, three of her priests entered. They looked at the Pope lying on the floor surrounded by vomit but did not react to the scene. Phaedra pursed her lips. As soldiers returned from the war, she knew they had seen much worse. Now, trained by her for the priest hood, they were unswervingly loyal.

"Father Gentry, hurry down to our doctors, only ours, and bring them. The Pope seems to have eaten something that doesn't agree with her." As she spoke, she pointed to the bowl of cheek meat.

"Father Brenner, set guards. No one is to enter or leave the seminary."

"Father Alomar, help me raise her eminence to the chair. We cannot leave her on the floor." With her eminence seated and unconscious, Father Alomar left taking the bowl of cheek meat with him.

Behind Phaedra, at the large open doors to the verandah, a breeze played joyfully with the drapes the let them hang limply once again.

In the chair, a large groan as Her Eminence struggled with vomit still dripping from the corner of her mouth.

"Help me..." she whispered.

Phaedra extended her foot and pushed.

"I already have, bitch!"

Elect-Si held the edge of the sheet close to her mouth and listened intently to Amunet beside her bed whispered into her ear so as not to wake Manuel. She turned her head to look at Amunet, a wide grin on her face. Slowly, she slipped out from under the sheets and took hold of her robe draped over the foot board.

Together they walked to the verandah to sit in the large spacious cushioned chairs.

Amunet drew her feet up onto the chair and hugged her legs, turning her face towards Elect-Si, she rested her head on her knees and smiled. Still being quiet, Elect-Si was rocking backward on the chair, smiling broadly and pumping the air with her fists. She kicked her feet in the air like a child who has just been told she has gotten a real pony for her birthday.

"The bitch is ours; she is ours! She is totally ours and will be for as long as she exists." Breathed Elect-Si. Slowly, she lowered her feet to the floor and stretched her fingers.

"You saw it, all of it? I don't doubt you, but this is too good! I never expected the vomiting to be as violent as it was. Sometimes gifts from the universe are better than you could ever imagine."

Amunet smiled and stopped hugging her knees as she sat back in the deep cushions.

"You have control Elect-Si, not your mother, nor any other vampire of your kind." She looked at her fingers.

"Your hands are on her throat now." She turned to look at Elect-Si.

"Sophyra is not immortal, like you, what you want to achieve with her must be done in the span of her life.

"Isn't that, right?" Asked Amunet as her face turned to the end of the verandah that was in darkness.

Elect-Si's head turned quickly to look at the far end to see a man, smartly dressed, step out of the shadows. Her hands became claws and her jaw dropped to allow her fangs to extend…

"N, no, it is all right; he is someone I know and love as a husband or a brother. He is Amun. He is the masculine to my feminine."

Elect-Si continued to watch the man with fierce caution, her fangs slowly slipped back into their sockets and her hands became less claw like.

"I am what Amunet says I am. I mean you no harm." The sound of Manual snoring suddenly interrupted the silence; Amun looked into the open doorway.

"I mean no one any harm."

"I told you the veil between the ethereal world and physical was becoming thinner, didn't I?"

Elect-Si looked past Amun and the open door; her guide was sitting like an elf on the verandah's wide stone railing. He looked at her and shrugged.

"This will happen!"

Elect-Si stood up and walked towards Amun.

"Amunet says I should not fear you, but I know Egyptian history; I have read the Pyramid Texts from the Old

Kingdom. You have not walked this earth since primaeval times."

Amun opened the cigarette caddy next to him. Slowly, he took out a cigarette and studied it before picking up a lighter and lighting the cigarette. He started at the place on her chest where her heart beat.

"Why are you here?"

"Amunet and I often talk about this world of humans. Of the world that creates, bends, and breaks the souls of those she receives at the doorway to the underworld."

Elect-Si met his stare and after a few moments of her challenging stare, he looked away at the tip of the cigarette.

"I want to walk in it as she does. As I used to. I want to feel the warmth of mankind's worship again. I want priest slaves to venerate me and sing my name in holy ceremonies. I want humans to labour at building temples to me. Is there anything wrong with this?" He looked at Amunet still sitting in the large chair.

"Amunet walks this earth with a fire dragon. I have no dragon." His voice was resonant and strong as he turned to look at her.

"You are Gatekeeper of Existence. Are you going to judge whether I can walk this earth, or not? Judge whether I can again be what I was and will become?"

Elect-Si looked to her guide. He looked impassively at her and then at Amun. He was waiting for her to make a decision. He turned his gaze away and looked at his feet.

"A decision must be enforced, remember that." His words were quiet, almost whispers, but they carried a weight she had never heard before from him.

"You must return to where you came from. I do not permit you to walk this earth. I do not permit you to speak to mankind. I do not permit you to touch the spirits and souls of mankind. This is my judgment." The solemnity to Elect-Si's words seemed penetrating and final in a way she had never expressed anything before.

Amun took a puff from his cigarette.

"And yet you will allow Amunet so much." He looked at Amunet still sitting in the large chair.

"This is not fair, Amunet, speak!"

Amunet shook her head.

"I no longer require anything of mankind. I do not require and do not want mankind to worship me. I do not want priest slaves honouring me. I need no one to sing my name. I need no sacrifices. I have not seen a temple for so long … so long that I no longer need one." Amunet stood up.

"I venerate what mankind has become. I worship them… I am not the Amunet you knew in the Old Kingdom. Yes, we talk … but you do not listen. You have heard the Judgment of the Gate Keeper," she looked at Elect-Si.

"It is final. You did not ask for fairness or balance. You asked for judgment, and you have been. This is the end."

Amun placed the end of the cigarette in an ashtray and straightened up to his full height.

Amun turned to Elect-Si and bowed then turned away and started to walk to the darkened end of the verandah, but before he reached it, he had faded away and was gone.

Elect-Si turned to Amunet.

"Do I need to be judged?" Asked Amunet.

Elect-Si felt a coolness and then an abrupt warmth pass through her body.

"Do I need to?"

"You should…"

Elect-Si's jaw stiffened as she looked into Amunet's eyes. The eyes of Amulet's fire dragon gazed lazily from her shoulder.

"I judge…" she paused, "… that all that you were, all that you are, and all that you will become require no judgment. Your fire dragon requires no judgment." She leaned forward and kissed Amunet on the lips.

"Walk where your spirit takes you, in this world, or in the world of spirits and different existences. The gate is open to you and your dragon for eternity … and all that comes after."

Amunet slipped her hand into Elect-Si.

"Amun asked for humanity to be subjugated to him. But he came up with another motive. The veil is slipping and you are the Gatekeeper, you will judge, and you will enforce. You will define how the worlds remain separated when the veil is gone. He wanted to see who and what you are. He wanted to see how you would judge a spirit trying to come into this world. Elect-Si, he came to judge you."

"Well, that was easy!" exclaimed her guide as he eased himself down from the railing.

"The next one may not be…" he looked at Amunet.

"You are very blessed," he faded into the darkness of the night.

From inside the room, Elect-Si heard her name being called. Amunet reached out to hold Elect-Si and returned the kiss. She smiled.

"Thank you. Now, get back in bed and fuck your human."

30. A Toast

Lady Challis poured a small measure of brandy into their crystal glasses and then added a slightly larger measure of chilled blood and sprinkles of a fine grind of herbs and spices.

She turned and handed a glass to her daughter. Elect-Si watched the spices and herbs slowly disappear below the surface and held her glass out for Lady Challis to toast with.

"I am not sure what we are offering a toast to," she looked past her daughter to Amunet, who held a glass of plain chilled water.

Amunet held her glass up for the toast.

"Elect-Si, Gatekeeper between the ethereal and spirit worlds and the physical world of man." Each of them sipped from their glass.

Lady Challis held up her glass,

"To judgment," she looked Amunet, and smiled appreciatively. Each of them sipped from their glasses.

Elect-Si held up her glass.

"To control of Pope Sophyra." They sipped from their glasses.

Gwendoline gave a small cough and held up her glass. "To my sister, for…." She paused, and looked at Elect-Si.

"For being your mother Elect-Si." She turned back to Lady Challis but did not sip from her glass; she swallowed the contents and threw the glass across the room. It landed in a deep corner of the colonial-style fire place and shattered.

"No one will toast with that glass … no one can do any better than the gift you have given us…"

She turned to look at Elect-Si, and bowed.

31.   To be. A Sister

Elect-Si pushed back the sheets and swung her legs off the bed. Across the large bedroom and out through the open verandah doors, the abundant flowers moved lazily in the night air. The clear night air allowed the stars to sparkle against a jet-black sky. She placed a hand over her heart and wondered at the infinite blackness that surrounded and protected her. Blackness before life in the universe started. The night sky might appear black but in comparison to what she felt, it was a lighter shade of grey.

Now, under her hand, she felt the brightness of light assert itself. Adding up the brightness of all the suns in the universe was like looking at an antique flashlight as the bulb dimmed and the batteries that powered it lost their energy. She had the white energy that powered all of those suns and so much more.

Lady Challis stared at the back of her daughter and gently rubber her hand over it. She slipped from under the sheets to sit beside her. She bushed some hair away from her shoulder and kissed it. She extended her fangs and gently passed them over the skin.

"You were so energetic last night… It was nice to have you back in my bed," she whispered. Her hand slipped down to her daughter's belly.

"I can feel her, you know that? It was another presence."

"Yes, I do. I am glad you can sense her. I wanted you to find out that way." She paused and put her hand over her mother and moved it slightly to be over the top of the growing fetus.

"There, do you feel that presence, she wants to be known by you?"

"Yes. Such energy, so young … so incomplete … but powerful." In a moment of silence, Elect-Si and her mother's breathing fell into sync.

"Is it Manuel's?"

"Yes."

"You two have been inseparable… On that subject. You need to make him one of us. You know that, don't you?"

"He could remain a human; he doesn't have to become a vampire."

"It would be better if he does. He will live longer, hundreds of years longer. Humans have such short lives. It may take your daughter hundreds of years to fully become what she will be. She should have a father and a mother." Lady Challis reached for her robe, stood up and slipped it on.

"If he stays human, he will be ashes long before she needs him." She walked over to the drinks cabinet and poured two glasses of water. Placing an ice cube in each. The small red ball of blood at the core of the ice cube would seep into and the water as the cube melted. She moved to the large comfortable chairs on the verandah. "New Moon, a Supermoon. Come. Look at it."

Elect-Si slipped on her robe and collected her drink and sat in a chair next to her mother.

"I hear you. But. I am worried." She paused and watched the ice cube slowly melt. It was at the point where it had melted enough that the small quantity of blood at its centre to start releasing and flavouring her drink. She sipped at the richness of the drink.

"I have bitten humans for food and kept them alive for months, sipping their blood as I needed it. I have bitten them to kill. I have never balanced my enzymes to make them one of us." She paused and looked up at Mars, a red ball hanging in the sky. A little further star gazing and she found Venus.

"I worry that I will bite him and kill him, or just give him a slow death."

Lady Challis looked at the profile of her daughter's face.

"When you think of balancing your bite, don't forget he has traces of venom from Ximena in his blood. She was one of Phaedra's kind." Lady Challis continued to stare at her daughter. She had said nothing about this added requirement.

"She could have transformed him into one of her kind. But she didn't" Elect-Si turned to face her mother,

"Maybe she knew best. Leave him as a human. They would have had only a short time together, but happy."

Lady Challis put down her glass on a small side table and folded her hands in her lap. She looked up at the stars.

"That is not our way; our kind does not do that. You know that. Think of him looking at you when you came back from Aldeburgh. As a human, he would be shocked, ashamed…"

"Horrified is the word you are looking for."

"Yes. As one of us, he would appreciate and understand what you did, and why."

"Yes… I see that."

"Elect-Si. Your body knows best. Bite him with the intention of making him one of us and that which makes you who you are will balance the enzymes. Trust in yourself. You are over thinking this."

"I love him and want him with me for as long as … eternity." The last word came out in a hushed tone. She had never spoken the words out loud, especially the last word.

Lady Challis chuckled, quietly.

"That is so obviously watching you two together. You even found a way to hold hands as we planned for Sophyra and Phaedra's visit. As to whether you can immortalize a human, I have no idea. I guess you will have to get to eternity and beyond to know whether you can or not."

"We will get to the end of eternity and look back together… You and me together."

"If you immortalize Manuel, there will be three of us."

"Isn't Gwen immortal?

" She is, but she will be off doing her own thing; she will look back on eternity in her own way. Just remember, when you bite, bite with the intention of what you want, what the outcome must be, your body knows, believe in it."

Lady Challis scanned the stars again and sipped on her drink. As she set her glass down, she reached into a pocket and took out a piece of paper. Slowly, she unfolded it and studied it.

"What is that?"

Lady Challis did not answer right away.

"It is the birth certificate for a baby girl. Brielle. The mother's name is Ximena, the father Manuel." She reached over and handed it to Elect-Si.

Elect-Si's face was impassive as she took the paper, but did not look at it right away.

"So… I am to be a step-mother?"
"Sister. We don't do Stepmother." Lady Challis finished her drink and stood up. As she looked down on Elect-Si, who was studying the birth certificate.

"Amunet is bringing her here as we speak. I had hoped to see them in the night sky."

Elect-Si folded the paper and slipped it into a pocket in her robe.

"Ximena was one of Phaedra's kind; they do not have wings so how is Amunet bringing her?" Elect-Si drained her glass and stood up to face her mother.

"Brielle has wings. My guess is that Ximena being impregnated by a human released a gene that allowed them to grow. I am going back to bed. Are you coming? But I want to sleep; you have tired me out."

"In a minute," said Elect-Si as she moved to the stone railing. In her mind's eye, images of a young girl on

Manuel's smartphone scrolled by. She started to wonder how she would be as a mother, sister, lover, and Gatekeeper of Existence.

"Better get some sleep as well; things are going to get busy!" she murmured to herself.

Elect-Si watched Brielle walk out on to the verandah. She liked her already. Black stilettoes, long athletic legs in tight leggings. A red athletic top under a leather jacket. The jacket was shaped and tight. The top was unzipped, revealing cleavage from high round breasts. Long black hair and olive skin. Almond shaped eyes from her mother's North Afrikan, Arabic heritage. She looked at Manuel with an expression of admiration for being Brielle's father but also a little surprised. This was No. 14-year-old; the person striding towards her was more like a mature twentysomething. Manuel smiled back and turned to look at his daughter with love and admiration.

"Vicereine!" The voice was clear, bright, and pleasant; it abruptly jerked Elect-Si's attention back to Brielle. For a moment, Elect-Si was a little lost. Where was the girl? Then she looked down. Brielle was kneeling on one knee in front of her, her head bowed. Long black hair clipped back with a simple gold hair clip.

"Brielle, stand up. Never, ever, bow to me. My name is Elect-Si. You must call me Si." Elect-Si extended her hand, which Brielle grasped as she stood up. It allowed Elect-Si to draw her into a loving embrace.

"So good to meet you." Whispered Elect-Si into Brielle's ear.

"So good to have you as my mother … it has been a long time without one." Whispered Brielle in return.

As the embrace loosened, Brielle placed a hand on Elect-Si's belly.
"A sister for me." She closed her eyes,

"She will be special … very special." She looked sideways at her father.

"As with me, my father's sperm will unlock something that needs to be here, in this world."

Elect-Si met Brielle's gaze as it returned to her.

"Any idea what that something special is?" But the question was met with a quick shake of Brielle's head.

"Wings, you have wings." Elect-Si turned to Amunet standing sipping water to one side.

"Scandinavia to Northern India in one night, Brielle is fast, very fast. Excellent use of thermals … she glides for very long distances. Saves energy."

"Meaning?"

"If you fly with her, you will have to work on your technique, or be left behind."

"You are losing your edge," said Lady Challis as she stepped forward.

Brielle moved to stand in front of Lady Challis and studied her for several long moments as if sizing up her ladyship. She slowly reached for, and then took hold of Challis's hand. The hand with the black diamond ring. She lifted it and held it between them before kissing the ring.
"My allegiance to you for eternity, and beyond, M'lady."

Lady Challis and Brielle hugged tightly.

Brielle leaned forward, her hands on her knees as she gasped for air. She had sprinted up the rock-laden path Elect-Si had pointed out as they flew over. Now, after almost daily visits, they were much higher in the Himalayas, the air was thinner, her legs burned and her heart beat as if it were trying to hammer its way out of her chest. At the end, the last 300 metres, she had been forced to leap from boulder to boulder as large blocks of ancient granite stood in her way. The thin air had not been a problem further down the trail, but now it seemed to limit her, test her, and take away her ability to do things she took for granted.

She stood up, wiping sweat and snot from her face and moved her tired legs, willing them to push her up the immense, steep, slab of rock to where Elect-Si sat watching her.

Finally, she sat next to her sister, her belly rippling like the bellows on an old metal forge.

"You made it! Congratulations."

Brielle looked down the face of the slab and the trail as it disappeared into the night.

"I will race you when you have delivered my sister."

"You are on!"

"Is this where you see the Yeti?"

"Yes. Listen, you can hear them; they are coming up slowly." Elect-Si pointed into the semi darkness of a first-quarter moon. Brielle turned to look in the direction Elect-Si pointed.

"Yes, I can hear them," whispered Brielle. A smile creeping across her lips.

"I can see them now; they are huge, much bigger than Hollywood makes them appear."

A group of Yeti emerged from behind a huge boulder: three males, taller and heavier than the females accompanying them, several small infants lagged and played behind them. They both watched in hushed silence as the Yeti meandered in and out of the boulders and disappeared into a gap between another large sheet of rock and the valley wall.

"That valley they went into is very narrow, but then it opens up. There are caves in which they live.

"Brielle, you have wings, there is more to it than Manuel, a human being your father isn't there?" asked Elect-Si.

"Yes, our species," she held up her slender but strong fingers and showed off her nails.

"We are one variant of the genus, vampire. You, another and Sophyra, another still. Sophyra's kind never had wings. You always have; most but not all our kind do. Phaedra is from one of the South American variants, and they have wings. " Brielle paused.
"Ximena would tell me our history, all the variants, those that had been successful and those that had not, and died out. Pure Darwin from the knee of my mother! She said some vampires from the great plains in what is today Argentina. They have wings, and fly great distances. Mother was from North Afrika. We are a mix of many smaller vampire species, Arabic, southern Afrika, and South American. I have the blood of a rare group of vampires from the deep deserts of Afrika. I have traits

from the eastern species of which your mother is the preeminent Goddess."

"On the female side, my grandmother, great-grandmother and those lost in time all came from deep deserts, Sahara, the Namib, and Kalahari. One very distant grandmother came from the Atacama in Chile, South America." Braille lay back on the rock and stretched out. The surface was oddly comfortable.

"We.... Rarely preyed on humans. Killing and feasting on human blood were a great delicacy. In the heat of the desert, blood is difficult to digest; you need to be well hydrated to process the iron rich liquid and animal meat is better than human. Water is more useful than blood." She extended her hands and looked at her nails.

"Scratching an animal, or a human, and injecting that way is much safer than biting. Fangs that can break. And the bite is close to the mouth, front claws, and hands of prey." She folded her hands over her stomach.

"Darwin would have called it natural selection, an adaptation to the challenges of our environment." She looked up at Elect-Si.

"Vampires are subject to all the same mechanisms of natural selection as humans, plants, and animals.

"I never looked at it that way. I have always thought of humans as just prey, and our way of injecting enzymes is the easiest. Today, we take many less than we used to," said Elect-Si.

"I tried biting a horse and a cow one time. But their skin was tough and the coarse hairs broke off in my mouth…" She laughed quietly.

"I was spitting out hair for hours afterwards."

Brielle sat up, resting her chin on her knees. She listened intently to the sound of rushing melt water and the screech of a night predator hunting for its food and killing it.

"Ask your mother, there was a time, tens of thousands of years ago, that vampires in Afrika had such long and stiff fangs that they could not fold back into their mouths. They walked around with them on the outside of their lips. I am guessing your fangs are shorter than Challis's, mostly because you do not need to go around biting horses and cattle." Brielle turned to look at Elect-Si.

"I would like to meet your Banjhakri, I think he has something to teach me!" Said Brielle.
"Are you immortal?" queried Elect-Si.

"I have a feeling you are, but..."

"Yes! Another trait in my species. I always find it odd that Hollywood portrays immortal beings as having a history that goes back to the beginning of time and extending to the end of it. But really, my immortality started 14 years ago when Mother gave birth to me." Brielle paused, and then slowly started to talk.

"Immortal at 14, but I have memories going all the way back to the first womb that carried my spirit. Mostly female but there are a few males; their sperm has to be strong and vile to carry male memories forward." She looked at Elect-Si.

"When I was born, I remember lying, all swaddled up next to my mother, her arm around me lying on the bed next to her in the hospital, the heart monitor, blood pressure, breathing all those things recording us. But all I could think of is how wonderful it was to be out of the womb and independent. Then all the faces appeared, faces of spirits … one, a few, and then a stampede. All the faces, all the vampires wanting to see the baby girl they had been born into. Then, one pushed through the crowd…"

"Sounds scary." Said Elect-Si, conscious she had not such memories.

"A vampire from the Karoo…she came right up to me and rested her hand on my forehead and suddenly the others started to disappear until only she was left. She explained she had given me the gift of stopping them from coming into my life until a time when I wanted or needed them. They would appear only on my terms." Brielle gathered some mucus in her throat and spat it out.

"I spend a lot of time with her, learning the old ways from her and how powerful I am, and how powerful I can be."

"You look a lot older, very mature … both physically and emotionally."

"Another adaptation. When you live in the desert, everything is prey to something else. You grow up quickly. You grow up very aware of everything around you. Even when you live in Lisbon."

"In the palace… Burkhardt…"

"I have already met him!" giggled Brielle.

"Next time you see him, he will have a split lip."

"He tried something?"

"He grabbed my ass. His lip ended up on the end of my left hook, and it split." Brielle paused for a moment and then turned to Elect-Si.

"I can sense immortal vampires. You, Challis, Gwendoline. Phaedra." Brielle looked down at her hands and then studied her finger nails.

"Another adaptation from the desert. An animal that knows it is going to die will often go to its den, or others of its kind. Tracking them on foot or in the air can result in more food. I can also make death horrifically agonizing. The prey feels as though their body is being burned from the inside out. Another Darwinian adaptation. Predators stay away from you if they know they will die a terrible death."

"Have you killed that way?" Elect-Si leaned back on her hands and studied her extended baby bump.

"Yes, just one."

"Yes. Well, more than a few. Humans. Witch doctors." Brielle studied Elect-Si.

"My kill was a vampire from the Argentina. He had flown to Lisbon to start a new life and spotted me shopping for fruit and vegetables. He followed me, and, in the night, he attacked me. I scratched him with the intention that he die horribly." Brielle paused; she looked around at the silvery light reflecting off wet rocks.

"He screamed so loud his vocal cords broke. All he could make were grunting sounds after that. He bled from every orifice until there was no blood left in him, then his heart stopped … so, I cut it out." Brielle continued to look at Elect-Si as if judging how the story was received. Happy with what she saw, she stood up and started to unfurl her wings. She held out a hand for Elect-Si to grasp to help her up.

"We should head back." She looked around at the tough landscape. She listened intently to the sound of rushing melt water and the screech of another night predator hunting for its food and killing it.

"I would like to meet your Banjhakri, I think he has something to teach me!" She repeated, as she finished speaking, she completed her preparations for flight.

As Elect-Si started to unfurl her own wings, Brielle drew close as if to whisper what she was going to say next. She held out her hands and wiggled her fingers playfully.

She turned away and started unfurling her wings before stepping off into the cool Himalayan air.

32.   Brielle meets a Banjhakri

Elect-Si landed. Her back was tired, her breathing was tired, where her wings attached to her body were tired, and her stomach was tired of supporting the baby. She felt her stilettoes sink into the damp soil. Mist was everywhere; it covered the ground in all directions and several feet from the edge of the forest. The sun would be up soon and it would burn off the mist. Behind her, she felt rather than heard Brielle land.

"He will be here soon enough; we just need to wait," murmured Elect-Si. She looked around and found a couple of large boulders that made something like an armchair. She sat down.

"So beautiful, so … so elegant. The way the mist covers the ground, the rocks, and the trees. Do you come often?" Asked, Brielle.

"Every few months. He is a teacher and a guide, a good one. But remember, he is a horny little bastard. Make sure you know where his hands are at all times."

Brielle eased herself on to a flat boulder and sat crossed legged, preening her wings.

"Message received."

Elect-Si heard Brielle's wings fold away. She thought, somewhat tiredly of doing the same with hers but gave up on the thought. She would preen when she was back at the palace. The baby was only a few days away from making its appearance. There was time. She rubbed her eyes and rubbed moisture from the mist on to her face and forearms, so refreshing.

"Is that him?" Whispered, Brielle.

"Yes."

The Banjhakri stood at the edge of the forest he was looking in their direction but seemed to be focused on Brielle. Slowly a grin spread across his face and his hands waved in the air excitedly. He moved quickly to the boulders where Elect-Si and Brielle sat.

"I can hear his thoughts," whispered Brielle excitedly.

Elect-Si turned to look at Brielle.

"I can hear both of you. Wow! This will be three-way telepathy…"

The Banjhakri stood in front of Elect-Si his hands fluttering in the air, his dark eyes sparkling.

"Of course, we can hear each other. Humans when they speak in a group, they hear each other. Why not us when we use our minds. Elect-Si is so good to see you." He turned to Brielle.

"You brought your sister and daughter." He used one hand to point at Brielle, the other to point at Elect-Si very pregnant stomach.

"She will be so special," he said, turning back to Elect-Si.

"You must not fly until after the baby is breathing on its own. It is such an incredible gift."

He moved closer and held out his hand, the fingers moving up and down in the air as a parent would try to catch the interest of their baby. He moved close and touched Elect-Si's stomach. As he did so, his eyes closed and he became very still.

"I can hear the thoughts of your baby," it was a statement rather than a question.

"I have heard her for several months. She is very intelligent, quick-witted, and strong-willed."

The Banjhakri nodded and moved back a few steps.

"Will you be ready for her when she arrives?"

"As ready as I can be… I have never known of a baby born with all the intelligence of its parents … will she be able to speak?"

"Of course! From the first minutes out of the womb. Why not?" His eyes turned to Elect-Si's breasts, which were full and heavy.

"Such breasts." He stepped forward quickly, his hands reaching out but her foot was quicker. It landed in the middle of his chest and stopped him moving any further forward.
"So unfair!" he exclaimed.

"There will be so much milk for the baby, why not some for little me?"

"All of it for the baby, none for you, that is final!"

The Banjhakri looked at her foot and after a moment moved back.

"Alright," he sighed.

"She will be born with the Toli you have. Time will have no meaning for her. The gate between the spirit world and this one, she will guard it with you. She will have…" he paused and turned to look at Brielle.

"She will be like you, and she will be like your other daughter."

"So, she will be immortal?"

"Did I say time will have no meaning for her!" He exclaimed.

"I am sorry, I forgot you need things repeated sometimes. The Toli, she will have the same power as you have."

"Why does she need something so powerful?"

"She will be a baby. If she does not have the protection you have, she will be prey for dark energies." He became thoughtful and looked up at Elect-Si.
"You have not been tested yet… Amun came to assess you, but he has not acted, nor has any of the other energies that desire to see the light of the sun." As his thoughts sank in, the first ray of sunshine broke through the mist and settled on his face.

Abruptly, the Banjhakri turned to Brielle.

"You came hoping for a gift…"

"I know you have a gift for me, but I am not sure if I will like it."

The Banjhakri shrugged and his face became clear and impassive.

"It is your gift, whether you like it or not. It must be given." He looked up at Brielle.

"You must scratch your father. You must make him one of your kind."

"Should I tell him?"

Elect-Si was surprised at the frankness and speed of Brielle's question. It seemed as though she was listening in on a conversation that had already started and was now coming to a conclusion.

The Banjhakri frowned and rolled his lips; his hands gestured in an uncoordinated way.

"Do you watch a snow flake fall from the sky; do you say to the snowflake, look out; you are about to land in a fire. No! You let it happen." His eyes locked on to Brielle's gaze.

"He already has some of your mothers in him. Give your gift as soon as you can."

Abruptly he turned back to look at Elect-Si. The sun was brighter now; he squinted to make eye contact.

"Your daughter will be twice blessed, twice armoured. She will have nails like your daughter here, and she will have fangs like you. She will be of both species." He seemed momentarily tired; he closed his eyes in deep thought.

"Yes, both species." He clapped his hands together, lightly at first, there was almost no sound. Suddenly, his clapping became much louder. He moved in front of Brielle and reached out for her thigh. As his hand landed on it, she gripped his wrist like a vice and pulled it away.

"You can speak without touching!"

His eyes opened in surprise. He tried to back away and as he did, an erection sprang from his fur. He struggled against her grip.

"I can try, can't I?" his voice in their minds was indignant. Finally, Brielle let go.

He looked at Elect-Si.

"You teach her too well." He looked at his wrist as if Brielle had hurt him, but he seemed more interested in how his fur had been squashed down and needed to fluff out. He breathed deeply and locked eyes with Brielle,

"Making your father one of your kind is your gift, but all human gifts come tied with a ribbon. Yours is to kill one of your kind … you know who she is she will pretend to be your mother's friend … but is actually her enemy."

Brielle nodded to the Banjhakri.

"I have already thought of that." As she spoke, she slid off the rock and suddenly reached for him and grasped his head by the fur surrounding his face and kissed him.

"Thank you for explaining my gifts; I thought there was only one."

His eyes lit up and he licked his lips.

"Are you sure I cannot fuck you?" As the words came out, his erection appeared again.

"I am sure." Smiled Brielle as she turned the Banjhakri around and pointed to his mate lurking at the edge of the woods.

"There, that is where you should take it.

" She looked down at his backward facing feet for a moment and then turned to Elect-Si,

"Si, if you are ready, we can fly home."

33.   A Baby is Born

xxx

Elect-Si looked up at the full moon; it bathed her on the day bed that had been pulled out onto the verandah and the crib next to her where her wonderful baby lay snoring. Her mouth stretched into a smile and her hand covered the laugh that always appeared when she remembered that special moment when Canasta had emerged from the womb squealing excitedly as if she were sliding down a water slide. It had so startled the doctor bringing her out that he almost dropped her.

An hour later, sitting in a comfortable chair, her belly still aching, and with Canasta lying in her lap, Elect-Si was astounded at the words coming out of the small mouth and the soft palate that could not quite from all of the words correctly. It was in a moment of frustration at not understanding what was being said that she first saw Canasta frown. Such tiny wrinkles and a squinting of the eyes. Canasta stopped speaking.

A terrible fear gripped Elect-Si in that moment. Had she said or given off a sense of frustration and anger at not being able to understand her daughter? Then she heard the words in her mind; they were clear, precise, and beautifully pitched.

"There aren't many mothers who can hear their babies speak an hour after birthing them!"

Elect-Si looked around; she was about to call out and ask who had said that. She was about to call out to the guards that were always present but discreetly hidden out of sight.

"Stop looking around, I am down here."

Elect-Si stared in disbelief at Canasta, her mouth starting to open in wonderment.

"Close your mouth, I can see your fillings … not nice mommy."

Elect-Si abruptly closed her mouth.

"Is that you Canasta?" she thought testing her ability to communicate using only her mind.

"Oh dear, I thought you were smarter than you seem to be. Look around, think around. How many telepathic vampires do you know? Hmmm, really! Of course, it is ME! Canasta. Your daughter."

"Telepathy…" blurted out Elect-Si in her mind.

"Yeah! You got it. When I grow up a bit, you will be surprised at how fast we can communicate that way. When my pallet firms up, we can have some good conversations. But we can also use our minds."

Elect-Si rubbed the spot on her chest over her heart.

"Your Toli, I was told…"

"Same as yours." There was a pause.
"I am immortal, like you. Just so you know." The thoughts paused again.

"Mommy, I am tired. I am going to sleep for a while. I will let you know when I want some milk."

Elect-Si stretched her legs out so they got the maximum amount of moonlight. With that Canasta rolled over, her eyes momentarily opened to look up at the full moon and she smiled. Closing her eyes, she went back to sleep.

"Surprising, isn't she?"

Elect-Si's head jerked around to her left. In a large cushioned chair, her guide sat comfortably, his legs stretching out to draw a foot stool closer to him so her could stretch his legs on it. Elect-Si noticed the cushions on the chair were showing a definite impression of someone sitting on them and her guide seemed fuller, more part of this physical world.

As if to confirm what she was thinking, her guide moved the cushions to adjust for the change in his seating position.

"Very well … you noticed the change."

"You seem to be more solid, more a part of this world, is that right. You are?"

"Correct. I can move things like the foot stool and I just love these cushions. It has been so many millennia since I felt cushions when I sit down."
"You knew Canasta would be telepathic."

"The thought crossed my mind; I hoped you would be too. If not, she would be alone in this world, well, the vampire world. Some humans are telepathic, but they have no control over it."

"Your presence in the physical world, is that changing the way we interact … as a guide?"

"Not in the slightest." He crossed his hands over his stomach as if considering what to say next.

"Amun. He is still planning to cross over when the veil is fully down. He wants to test you. He is a spirit of action, carrying out deeds of great prowess."

"I have no sense of the veil and of the other worlds. I need you to tell me when the veil drops."

"I know you don't sense the veil. But you will know when it drops, you are the Gatekeeper. You will feel the change.

"Canasta's mind is so incredibly strong already, such a weapon … such an incredible weapon." He looked at Elect-Si with a look that told her he was about to impart something that was important.

" She has your Toli; she is infinitely protected." Her guide looked away, studying the wall decorations and the lightly moving drapes.

"Brielle, she is protected by something like you, but different. Let's leave it at that." He unclasped his hands and held on to the arms of the chair and slowly pulled himself up. As he stood tall, he faded away.

For a long moment Elect-Si stared straight ahead, unmoving, frozen with the information she had just received. A memory of meeting with Amun floated into her mind; he stood smoking a cigarette, complaining about humanity not worshipping him and how he so wanted the human race to be subjugated and grovelling in the dust before him.

Elect-Si turned her attention to the moon hanging silvery and pure against the black sky of the night. Her sharp vampire eyes caught a small flicker of white light, the tiniest of stars like shimmers on the surface. Humans were on the moon, there was a small colony, 250 people, some had been there for more than a year and were due to be back on earth at the end of the month. She tilted her head to one side and rested her chin on the back of her hand.

Challis would be at the space centre to meet them and spend time with the astronauts who were also vampires. As humanity went out to colonize space, vampires would go with them.

Mars was next.

The launch for Mars, in three months.

34.   Giving a Gift

Manuel looked up from the potting bench as Brielle walked into the large greenhouse.

"Just look at this place; it is as big as the Victorian-glass houses at Kew Gardens in England. And to think they refer to it as a potting shed!" He straightened up and pressed his hands to his back to remove the stiffness.

Brielle walked over slowly, taking time to look at the richness of the plants and even the Palm trees soaring thirty and forty feet above her and still not touching the glass roof.

"This is a Victorian, isn't it? I mean the glass house."

Manuel looked around and nodded.

"Yes, built a little after Kew Gardens, a slightly bigger scale but, of course, the British of the era would not hear of an Indian Maharaja building something bigger so they never acknowledged it."

Brielle walked up to Manual and hugged him. You must be very happy," she smiled at her father.

"I am very, very happy." He looked at his daughter with a serious expression on his face.

"What makes me even happier is that you and Elect-Si are getting along so well. Do you really like her? This has been such a rush, coming here, learning about the different kinds of vampires and the schemes they play on each other."

Brielle rubbed her father's arms.

"Don't forget, you and Elect-Si banging it away between the sheets and now I have a really cute, amazing baby sister."

"We have not talked in depth about Elect-Si and me, or about how Canasta came so quickly to the relationship. Are you sure you are OK about it?"

"Papa, I have told you many times, and I have told Si, I have told Anastasia, I have told Wellington, I have even told the footman. Yes! I am happy for the both of you." She passed her father a short piece of bamboo he gestured for.

"Ximenia, I would not have wanted you to live alone. You have me, but that is not the same as having a wife and mother in your bed next to you. You need Si and she needs you. Be comfortable with that! Please… Please do not ask again."

Brielle watched her father measuring and drawing lines on the bamboo as he prepared to make a climbing lattice for a plant that likes to climb and grow on a frame.

"Have you been able to communicate with Canasta?"

"Yes." Brielle paused as her father started cutting and splitting the bamboo into strips with a machete.
"She has a very sharp mind and is totally aware. Aware of the world, her Toli, of the schemes going on, her mother, her father, and of course, what she is."

"Jealous?"

"No, on the contrary, it affirms who I am and where I came from. Sometimes when I am meditating, I can see my life path, where I am going, and why. I know now, more than ever, who I am."

Brielle watched as the strips her father was cutting and trimming. The longer strips were becoming even more flexible and bent often.

"That will be a very fine lattice when you are finished."

She had always admired and loved her father for his ability to make things rather than go out and buy what he needed. When she had been very young, she remembered him repairing her tricycle when a wheel came off. Something other fathers seemed incapable of doing, which gave her an immense sense of pride.

She knew he was different from her mother in a very important way, but it was at her sixth birthday party that she found out. A mean-spirited son of a family friend told her in a corner of the garden. At first, she denied it but then she realized it was true … her mother was a vampire, like all the other families and their children, but her father, Manuel, was something less; he was human.

In bed that evening, she had been looking up at the starry night painted on her ceiling by her father and had burst into tears as she retold the words she had heard, and asked why her mother was married to a human. Could she not scratch him and make him one of their kind, she had asked? Why did all the other parents and children know but she didn't? Why was her mother not doing things that made common sense and would protect Manuel?

Ximenia had tried to explain. But words had not been what she wanted to hear. They seemed to reinforce the fact her father was not a vampire and that made her sad and the tears had started to flow. Anger started to flow. Frustration flowed and a little fear that something might happen to her father, the repairer of tricycles, painter of her ceiling, and the grower of living things. She pounded on her mother's shoulders with her small fists. Finally, as she lay down on her bed, she told her mother that if she would not scratch Manuel and make him a vampire, she would.

Her mother had gotten angry. Very angry. She had told her she was too young to know how to balance the enzymes in her scratch. She did not know the right recipe; she had called it. The fine difference between killing a human, making them your servant for feeding, and making them a vampire was a balance.

Her had become very stern and a little frightened in that moment. She had made Brielle swear an oath, an eternal oath, that she would never scratch her father.

A year later, her mother was dead, taken from the family by some evil humans. Her father had been injured in the attack; she had watched from a small bathroom window as her father defended her mother but was finally beaten unconscious.

After that she had grown very close to her father as they moved from house to house, trying to be unknown and unknowable. A bereaved father and daughter seeking quietness and peace.

Finally, out of desperation and fear that she might face the same fate as her mother, he had journeyed to visit Lady Challis to ask for help. Her ladyship was a mythical being, an immortal vampire of such immense power, and incredible abilities. No one, no matter what kind of vampire, truthfully knew if she even existed. But her father knew and he asked for help for both of them.

When Manuel returned with news and stories of the visit, and how he was treated, where they would be moving to and how they would be protected, she lay awake in bed fearful and excited at the same time.

A few days later, she had looked out of her bedroom window at her father down on the verandah pressing soil around the stem of a plant and adding generous amounts of water. A ping sound on her tablet announced the arrival of an email from a friend where she had lived. She read and reread it in disbelief.

The people who had killed Ximena were not humans, they were vampires of a different kind than her mother. They were all dead. Their families were all dead. Cars had crashed and burned, houses engulfed in fire, and several drowned when their boat overturned when they were out fishing. Three out hiking had inexplicably fallen off high rocky paths, and eaten by animals.

Brielle had covered her mouth as she put her tablet down. All the accidental deaths had happened within days of each other. But she felt they were not accidents; they were an act of judgment; those who had died had all been tried and convicted by something far greater than they could comprehend.

"Oh fuck!"

The words brought her mind skating back into the now. Her father was holding his hand, trying to stop it shaking. One of the slender, sharply pointed bamboo stalks was sticking out of the side of his hand. His face contorted in pain.

"I was trying to bend it around that large stick and the bamboo cracked and sprang back on me." He snorted at the pain caused by the lattice he had been building moving in the table top.

"It goes right through and comes out there. Oh shit, now it is bleeding."

"We have to cut the stalk and pull what is left and pull it out."

"You know best Brielle. Tell me what you have to do." Brielle picked up a pair of pruning shears and held her father's hand.

"I am sure this will hurt. After, we can get you to the palace doctors."

Her father nodded his approval. Suddenly, he cursed violently. Brielle had cut the bamboo.

Brielle held her father's hand as he brought his breathing under control and waited for his eyes to open.

"There is a splinter in the wound. I can feel it." He met her gaze.

"You will have to take it out."

Brielle stared at the bleeding wound. Yes! she could see the splinter; it was larger than she thought would be left behind. She picked up a small knife and then looked at her father.

"I will have to get my nail into the wound and use this knife to help pull the splinter out."

"I know baby, I know it will hurt." Their eyes met.

"I trust you." He nodded, and breathed deeply.

"Get to it. Get it done."

As he spoke, Brielle concentrated hard, focusing her intention and her mind, and slowed her breath. Then she took a deep breath and monetarily closed her eyes to focus again and then pushed her thumb nail into the open wound. A stream of clear fluid with a very specific purpose came for her nail into his blood stream as she eased her nail in deeper. Her father's blood ran down it onto her hand.

Slowly she levered the splinter up so its bloody tip pointed up at her. Her father cursed loudly. She brought the point of the knife down on the splinter and started easing it out along her nail as the wound became increasingly bloody.

"It's out!" exclaimed Brielle as she tore a piece of fresh white cotton from her shirt and wrapped it around her father's hand. She held his face and kissed his cheek.

"You are so brave. It is all done. Everything is done. Everything will be fine now. Everything. Come Papa. We must go to the doctors." She took his good hand and began leading him out of the glass house.

35.   A Pope Arrives

Pope Sophyra sat slumped unhappily in a large chair overlooking the reflecting lake. Her mood was dark, her face covered in a scowl, her arms limp. She wore little makeup, loose strands of hair moved in the gentle breeze that came in off the water. Her Papal attire seemed as disorganized as her mood.

Behind Pope Sophyra, Phaedra puffed on a cigar. She looked down on the top of Pope Sophyra's head with a stare that could have bored a hole right through the skull like a laser.

"Her sexual appetite has grown considerably since injecting the enzymes. I am not sure why." Phaedra looked up at Lady Challis and Elect-Si.

"I make sure every priest I put in front of her is castrated. There won't be another pregnant Pope."

Pope Sophyra leaned forward slowly, scowling.

"I am still Pope in the East. I still have power; I still have loyal priests and bishops of my kind ... my kind." She waved her hand as if to emphasis the fact.

"They will do what I say when I want them to. You both will pay for doing this to me!" Her voice was shrill and almost a scream. As she stopped speaking, she slumped back into the chair.

"I have a right to my sexual appetites. I will continue to exercise them as my needs demand."

Lady Challis looked at Phaedra, a questioning expression on her face.

"All of her kind that we can identify are being, or have, shall we say, been neutralized." Phaedra exhaled a large puff of smoke.

Elect-Si glared at Pope Sophyra and slowly brought her hands together and rested her chin on them.

"We were to have control, not a zombie. What did you do exactly?"

"We have to work with the result." Interrupted Lady Challis glaring at Elect-Si.

"My guess is you gave Sophyra an overdose."

Phaedra slowly started grinning. It disappeared in a moment, though.

"I made sure the Fang was empty. That's all. No one said anything about dosage when I left here."

"She will do what we want; that is the main thing … the only thing." She looked down at Sophyra.

"Baby, would you like a priest, a quick fuck before dinner? I brought your favourite with us."

Sophyra turned to look up at Phaedra and nodded.

Phaedra beckoned to two servants.

"Take her to her suite and make sure Father Ambrose is there. Lock the door."

As soon as the chair was empty, Phaedra moved around and slumped into it, a broad smile on her face, she puffed heavily on the cigar. She looked from Lady Challis to Elect-Si and back…

"What?"

36.   Persephone

Burkhardt stood by the elegant, richly plated dinner table, a slight breeze coming in across the open dining room from the reflecting lake. He seemed elegant, but Lady Challis noted the whips of grey in his hair as she walked over to him.

"It has been a long time since you have been in my bed," whispered Lady Challis as she stood facing him.

"M'lady, please forgive me … family duties keep me away from your arms." He turned to look at her.

"Si knew what she was doing when she passed judgment. I have never been you so emotionally happy and drained of energy at the same time." Their eyes met.

"I would love to be back in your bed, fulfilling my duty."

"Duty! Is that what fucking me is now? I thought it was a pleasure you looked forward to … we looked forward to." She scolded him.

"I didn't mean it that way. A bad choice of words." He stammered.

"I know what you meant; I am just playing with you.

"As the words came out slowly, her hand drifted down his chest, stomach, and finally his crotch. She could feel the stiffening penis through the dress pants and smiled.

"At least my being close to you still makes you hard." She paused,

"Are the servants at each station and with each guest, they are from Miray's Special Forces?"

"Yes, armed, and armoured. There will be no one coming in or out of the room that is not from one of her team. The Palace and the surrounding area are on lock down and heavily patrolled. Drones are in the air; the palace complex has been swept twice for explosives and dangerous substances."

"Everything is recorded, video, audio, heart rate, lie detectors … everything."

"Yes, and tested."

Lady Challis took her hand away from Burkhardt ragingly stiff penis.

"Good." Their eyes met.

"It would be good to have you in me again, when you can find the time."

He smiled.

"After dinner, I can think of no better desert than to hear you scream as I make you come."

"After dinner it is…"

Lady Challis looked to her left. Pope Sophyra was making a grand entrance, a cream, red and gold sari with a gold crucifix on a chain that was a little too heavy for it. Her Cardinal's ring is visible on one hand, the Papal ring on the other.

Burkhardt moved quickly to her side to offer her his hand and guided her to her seat. He had to turn quickly to meet Phaedra, who was now standing at the entrance.

Dressed in a flowing full-length black and white panelled leather dress with a white strapless bustier emblazoned with crucifixes made from white and yellow diamonds. A crucifix covered in rubies rested proudly on her cleavage.

Elect-Si appeared at the entrance but did not wait for Burkhardt. She walked to her seat and adjusted her simple grey leather jacket and knee-length skirt. A pale blue leather bustier, with matching stilettos. Her waist length black hair was restrained in a series of plain gold hair clips. On her ring finger, a diamond eternity ring signified her marital status.

Lady Challis watched as her daughter engaged in idle chatter with the Pope and Phaedra, who now seemed wildly overdressed.

Phaedra played with the knives and forks at her place setting.

"I find it rather human for you to wear a ring on your wedding finger. After all, vampires do not marry … we, ah, mate. Manuel is a human, you, you are immortal, he will be dead, and dust before you even notice."

Elect-Si locked eyes with Phaedra, and stretched out her hand on the table cloth so all could see the ring.

"It is an infinity ring; it symbolizes never-ending love."

At the entrance to the room, there was a distinct clip of hard heels that drew their attention. Brielle stood there, waiting for Burkhardt. A simple gold chain at her neck, a loose white silk camisole top on thin straps. A. Wellington era Hussars dress uniform jacket resting casually over one shoulder, dress uniform pants with gold brocade at the sides, and black leather boots with spurs on her feet.

Phaedra's nostrils flared as she looked at Brielle. She watched as Burkhardt led her to the seat next to Elect-Si. She visibly sniffed the air as Brielle placed her jacket on the back of her chair.

"I understood everyone at the table was to be unarmed. Your daughter has a dagger strapped across the small of her back!"

Brielle turned to look briefly at Phaedra to let her know that she had heard. She turned back to her jacket and took it from her chair and pretended to remove some specks of cotton from the elaborate brocade, and then placed her jacket back on the chair and adjusted to several times. Finally, she sat down and stared at Phaedra without speaking. With her finger nail, she tapped her crystal glass and waited for it to be filled. She took her eyes away from Phaedra as she held the glass up to examine the colour of the wine.

"The terms agreed for this dinner did not say anything about weapons of heritage. A dagger is part of my heritage." She smelled the wine and then sipped from the glass. As she set the glass down, she looked into Phaedra's angry eyes.

"Go fuck yourself!"

Lady Challis brought her serviette up to cover the smile spreading on her lips. Brielle was definitely growing up on her; she liked Brielle, she decided. She waved to Burkhardt to start serving dinner.

As she put down her serviette, she realized that Brielle was her granddaughter. She had never thought of her this way before. Vampire lineage did not require a consummated blood line the way humans did. Being a vampire was the blood line, Canasta, and Brielle were both her grandchildren. As she felt the warmth of her feeling towards Brielle and Canasta growing. She looked down on her plate and slowly picked up her knife and fork.

"Are you going to allow that?" Blurted Phaedra angrily.

"I should rip out her nails!"

Lady Challis slowly cut into her venison and used her knife to layer a small number of mashed potatoes on to her meat. She looked up at Phaedra refusing to add anger to her stare.
"Brielle is my granddaughter … touch her and you touch me!" She put her food into her mouth and slowly ate. Her eyes fixed on Phaedra. She dabbed at her lips with her serviette as she swallowed.

"If you dare to do that… I will purge this planet of your species. Do you understand?" Lady Challis sipped from her wine.

"You don't have to say anything … just speak and act appropriately while I let you live."

"You can't do that!" Scowled Phaedra.

"Burkhardt, papers, do you have the papers?"

"Yes, M'lady."

"Give Phaedra the copies."

"Of course."

Burkhardt moved to the serving cabinet, from a safe in the elegant furniture; he took a grey folder. He placed it on a silver serving platter and brought it to Phaedra.

She stared at the folder for several seconds before picking it up gingerly, as if the folder were dangerous.

Phaedra started reading the top paper and then briskly looked through the others. She threw the folder back on to the serving platter and indicated Burkhardt could take it away.
He looked at Lady Challis for instructions. She shook her head.

"Phaedra will be taking them with her; she has to show them to an old man, a gardener at her seminary, whom she calls father." Said Brielle.

"For years it was believed your mother's death was at the hands of humans who learned what she was. Not so. Her killers were led by a faction of Phaedra's species controlled by that old man."

Elect-Si moved to place her hand on Brielle's forearm. As Brielle moved to try and break free, Elect-Si strengthened her grip; she looked at her daughter.

"No!"

"Did you read the last pages? You should. It is a report. My people together with a few trusted humans hunted the killers. Those confessions were extracted under extreme duress." Lady Challis cut another piece of venison and added some blood-sauteed onions to the mashed potatoes on her fork.

"The last pages describe the tracking of each killer's family, extended family members, close friends, and acquaintances. The final list is when they were executed."

She placed the food into her mouth and ate. As she finished, she taped her glass to be refilled.

"I believe you call them blood lines in your species... Lisbon has 14 fewer now."

Lady Challis looked at a livid Brielle.

"Phaedra did not kill your mother. But I have ensured the blood lines of all responsible have been wiped from the earth." Said Lady Challis.

Slowly, Brielle brought her anger under control and turned to stare at her plate. Slowly, she picked up her utensils and started eating in silence.

"Elect-Si, what do you want done?" The question was asked in hushed tones, the words cut across the table but split the atmosphere. The voice was unmistakable; it was Pope Sophyra.

Elect-Si looked up to acknowledge Pope Sophyra and put down her utensils; she patted her lips with her serviette all the while looking at Pope Sophyra.

"How are we to address you in private?"

"Sophyra will be sufficient. I..." she hesitated.

"The harvesting of humans is over... I determined Dorion was to blame." Snapped Elect-Si.

Sophyra looked crestfallen; her apology, obviously carefully crafted, over several days since she arrived, had been taken away from her.
"Dorion saw a weakness in your kind and exploited it. I speak of the lover of excess." Elect-Si indicated to Burkhardt that she was finished with her plate.

As the servants replaced the first course with those required for the second, Burkhardt set a simple vinyl binder to one side Sophyra's second course.

"A little light reading before, after, or instead of using Father Ambrose. It is a tally of all the bodies shipped back from the war, as well as gold, diamonds, rubies, sapphires, and rare earth minerals." Elect-Si stared across the table.

"Phaedra knows about this, on the last page … uranium. To make dirty bombs, is that not so."

"Uranium?" Asked Sophyra to look at Phaedra.

"To make such bombs, yes. A safety measure in case humans discovered us… All! Of us." Said Phaedra, leaning forward and looking around the table for emphasis.

"The shipment didn't arrive. The containers slipped off a cargo ship during a storm."

Elect-Si looked down at her soup course; she sprinkled some blood flakes on it. After a moment, the flakes sucked up moisture from the broth and turned into the most elegant little beads of glistening, liquid blood. She broke them easily with her spoon as she swirled the contents of her bowl.

From across the table, there was the sharp, dangerous sound of a spoon dropping on to precious antique China.

"This page purports to show how much Dorion was skimming off the shipments for her own use. This is outrageous!" Exclaimed Sophyra

Phaedra played with the remaining utensils at her setting.

"How do you think your basilica in the capital was paid for after you passed that edict about church finances?" A hardness appeared in Phaedra's lips, and a muscle twitched on her jaw.

"That was her gift to you."

"To me!" Blurted out Sophyra.

"I have yet to step inside to lead services for the poor."

"Poor! Poor! Did you say Poor?" Asked Phaedra as she tapped Sophyra's plate.

"The poor do not eat off gold plates and drink from challis encrusted with rubies and diamonds." Phaedra sipped at her soup.

"Are you going to stop castrating young men?"

"I already have… If you had paid any attention to the seminary while visiting it, you would have found that out."

Sophyra beckoned for her soup to be taken away. "All those fighters coming back from the war, they go straight to your seminary and then the priesthood. They are a cadre of unswervingly loyal followers, aren't they?"

Sophyra remained silent for a few moments.

"The first night I used Father Ambrose, he called your name as he came."

Phaedra visibly bit her lip to stop herself from laughing out loud.

"If that is the case, why are you still with him?"

"Because I am better than you. My kind is better than yours. We are more capable, and never forget, our venom is more poisonous than yours. We are, in all ways, superior." Sophyra sat back in her chair as the next course was being served.

"Never, ever, forget Phaedra."

Phaedra stared straight across the table; her eyes focused on nothing in particular.

"I know what I know. Dorion gave me a report and a laboratory analysis." Snapped Sophyra.

Phaedra snorted.

"You believed her! No lab report can provide details of how venom enters a body, how it changes it and how it kills."

Sophyra broke off a succulent flake of fish and added some bloody marinara sources to it. She scooped it into her mouth.

"Sophyra, Phaedra, we expect you each to forgo uranium weapons, now, and always. We expect to have a delegate at the venom tests." Stated Elect-Si.

"Agreed!" Sophyra's words came quickly and with a sharp edge to them.

Agreed! Said Phaedra firmly, staring harshly at Elect-Si.

"Did you not make a pledge of loyalty to me? I spoke for both of us; that means you and me."

"One of the good things about Dorion was her penchant for writing things down. Read it. It binds you, and your kind to me."

Phaedra froze. Could she have gotten so far in pursuit of her ambitions that she had made a fatal error? Had she bound herself and her kind to a stupid, arrogant bitch from a species like Sophyra.

Burchardt stood with a lighted wood match for Lady Challis to light her cigar with.

She turned to face the room as she listened to Miray reporting on her audit of nuclear weapons accumulated during the human war period. Miray had been thorough as always. Weapons counted, viability assessed, old or outdated security systems replaced. Additional layers added, exhaustive background checks on all involved, rotation of guards and personnel. Intrusion tests. Even a mock assault test on one weapons bunker located on an out-of-the-way island in the Pacific.

As Miray paused, she looked at Lady Challis.

"Keep going, there is more." Miray nodded. Information on new bunkers being built to accommodate weapons from stores that might be vulnerable to detection.

Sophyra had agreed to give up uranium to make dirty bombs far too easily, which made Challis all the more wary of her.

Nation states had a habit of losing a nuclear weapon here and there. But no weapon was really lost; Pope Sophyra had them! She had more than enough to destroy the planet.

Lady Challis picked up an ash tray and knocked ash from her cigar into it.

"Spies. Intelligence. Miray, we need to know everything about Sophyra and Phaedra and their species. We need to protect ourselves." Said, Brielle.

"The venom tests, of Sophyra and Phaedra's kind, compared to ours, take us into the realms of biology and biological warfare."

Lady Challis looked at her granddaughter and puffed on her cigar. Such awareness and ability to speak her mind.

"What are you thinking?"

"Could tests be used to create a way to negate each of our species' ability to create new vampires or feed and kill humans?"

"Your venom is different from Phaedra's but that may be because of your father was human. We are testing venom from the Saharan coven you sent us to." Said Miray.

Lady Challis stared for a moment at Brielle.

"And."

"Evolution, Darwin taught us evolution, survival of the fittest takes a long time but human intervention takes a few years." Brielle smiled thinly.

"Challis, you may be more at risk than my kind. Fanged vampires have been on earth since the dawn of time. I so loved hearing about when you met Lucy and made friends with her." Brielle turned to her mother.
"If they found a way to stop our venom from killing, or binding a human to us for feeding, or siring vampires, all that are living would be the last of each of your species."

Lady Challis raised an eyebrow. Such thinking and only yesterday they had celebrated her 15th birthday. She closed her eyes. A memory floated into her mind's eye. A Nazi banner hanging from a tall stone wall moved slowly in a cold breeze from an open window.

She looked down at her stunningly shiny black-jack boots. The red armband with its swastika called out brightly from her black SS uniform. In her left hand she held the cap of an SS-Gruppenführer und Generalleutnant der Waffen-SS. The eyes of the Death's Head insignia on her cap seemed to be alive and intelligent. It seemed to know what was about to happen.

She looked again at the cage in the corner of the room, a small boy, a vampire, starved, naked. Beaten and covered in dirt and his own feces. Chained at the neck, hands, and ankles. Sitting on old dirty straw. Shivering from the cold coming in through the window. Mouth horribly mutilated, fangs cracked and exposed.

She had seen, and heard enough.

Slowly she raised her cap and placed it on her head, a signal to her team. Her right hand drifted to the Sturmgewehr 44 over her right shoulder. Abruptly she swung it up into both hands. She squeezed the trigger. The submachine gun erupted violently. Her guards did the same. Bullets chewed up tables, chairs and smashed glass beakers spilling their contents. Everyone in the room, every scientist, every assistant was killed…. But, to make sure, while her team secured research papers and set incendiary and demolition charges, she walked around the room with a strange dedication, shooting each body in the head with her Luger pistol. Just to make sure. The boy was carefully removed; he would be going with her to safety.

At a vantage point overlooking the old castle, she had her driver stop so she could watch it erupt into violent flames, Walls cracking and it collapsed as more explosions tore through it.

"Miray, in the library, we still have papers from that Nazi era castle and the experiments they were doing on that young vampire boy during WWII. Have them translated and their value assessed." She looked at Brielle.

"Maybe you can help with that." Said Elect-Si reaching for her drink.

"We must manage humanity with more diligence and care; they are a resource. They are food and fruit, and when we convert them, new vampires to supplement our breeding." Mused Lady Challis. She looked at Brielle as she sipped from her glass.

"You and I will work to understand how our genres can work together against Sophyra and Phaedra."

"Burkhardt, execute that old gardener." Said Lady Challis looking at her cigar.
"Thank you, Anastasia. I appreciate that." Smiled Brielle. Then she raised her glass.

"I look forward to working with you on those old papers."

"Who is he again?" Said Brielle pointing past Lady Challis.

Elect-Si turned to look where her daughter pointed.

Her guide sat on one of the spare chairs lined up against the wall. He smiled and gave Elect-Si the thumbs up. As their eyes met, his gesture changed to a finger-pointing to the right. Elect-Si's eyes followed the direction he pointed and came to a very elegant, Grecian-looking woman with tanned skin, large almond eyes, and long black curly hair. Even as a woman, Elect-Si considered her to be very attractive.

She was wearing a white toga, gold necklace, bracelets, rings, and decorated brown leather sandals. She moved to a chair at the back and sat down resting her chin on the back of her hand. She was looking directly at Elect-Si. Her presence was clear and solidly in this physical world in so many ways that Amun had not.

"Hello Elect-Si, I am Persephone." She said.

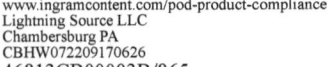